The Brutalis

Chapter 1 - The One That Walked Away

The pavement was wet, but it hadn't rained.

Just fuel. Oil. Something slick and black that clung to Kris's palms as he dragged himself forward on shattered knees.

Smoke curled around his ears like it wanted to whisper something.

But there was no sound.

His ears were ringing — a high, piercing drone that had swallowed everything else. No sirens. No shouting. No traffic. Just the shriek of surviving something you weren't supposed to.

He didn't turn around.

Didn't need to.

The heat behind him was enough — the kind that made your teeth ache and the hair on your arms rise like it was begging to catch fire next.

Glass bit into his hand. He kept crawling.

One shoe gone. Jacket burned open across the side. A line of blood marked the concrete behind him like a broken tail. His right eye wouldn't open fully. Smoke had kissed it too close. His throat burned like he'd swallowed the explosion instead of outrun it.

A shadow moved. Not help. Just a bystander with a phone.

Kris didn't wave. Didn't ask.

Just got to his feet — somehow — and stumbled toward the alley between the off-license and the shuttered betting shop. His shadow danced beside him, taller than it had any right to be.

Every step felt like it didn't belong to him.

Legs of borrowed meat. Ribs that clicked when he breathed.

A cat darted past. No sound. Just shape and teeth and gone.

He touched the wall as he walked. Needed it.

Needed something solid because the world was beginning to tilt.

The sky had that grey, pre-dawn colour — the one that doesn't admit what time it is. Could've been 4 a.m., could've been the end of everything.

He stopped once. Leaned forward. Spat blood into the drain.

Then he kept walking.

Left hand shaking. Right hand clutched around nothing.

He didn't look back.

The alley was dead quiet except for the buzz of a flickering streetlamp.

It made everything look green. Sickly. Cheap. Like the world was being filmed on CCTV.

Kris ducked into the shadows and dropped his weight against a metal fire door that didn't open. He slid down until he was seated on the cold concrete, chest heaving like he'd run a mile on broken legs.

He peeled back the ripped half of his shirt. The wound on his side was jagged, blistering, black around the edges. Something had torn through — not a clean break, not a bullet. Just fire and shrapnel. His blood was sticky. He pressed his palm to it.

In the silence, his breath came out louder than usual — ragged, deep, like someone learning how to live again. He reached into the inside pocket of what was left of his jacket and pulled out a burner phone.

Charred edges. Screen cracked. But it still worked.

It buzzed once.

Unknown number.

He stared at it for a long time, thumb hovering.

No name. No message.

Just that buzz — like a warning, not a call.

Kris didn't answer.

He didn't even unlock it.

He stood slowly, limping toward the nearest bin, and dropped the phone inside without a word.

It hit the trash with a quiet clunk — nothing dramatic. No one noticed.

Behind him, a skinny dog nosed its way out of the shadows. Pale coat. Eyes like coins left in bleach.

It stared at him.

Kris stared back. Said nothing.

The dog didn't bark.

Didn't flinch.

Just stood in place, watching him like it was waiting for the next scene.

Kris turned. Walked out of the alley.

The dog didn't follow.

He passed three closed shops and a newsagent with all the lights still on but no one inside. A soft hum of electricity. Fluorescents. Neon beer signs. The whole street felt like it had been abandoned mid-sentence.

Kris lit a cigarette with the hand that wasn't shaking.

Held it between lips that didn't part.

And kept walking.

Kris stepped into the off-license like he belonged there.

The bell above the door didn't ring. It was missing. Just a bit of frayed wire swinging in the metal bracket.

Fluorescent lighting flickered overhead — too white, too loud. The place smelled like spilt Lucozade and stale bread. Nobody at the till. The door was unlocked. Maybe someone had just left the place to rot overnight.

Behind the counter, a small flatscreen TV was bolted to the wall.

No sound.

Just images.

Footage looped from a helicopter view — fire crews hosing down a twisted frame of metal that used to be a car. Black smoke smeared the sky. Police cordons like red stitches on grey streets.

Kris stood still, watching it. Face unreadable.

No headlines.

Just the crawl:

BREAKING: East London Explosion – Two Presumed Dead – No Names Released

His reflection looked thin in the glass fridge door.

Ashes on his face. Cuts up his neck.

One eye half-shut. The other — distant. Cold.

He grabbed a bottle of water. Didn't open it.

Pulled out a note from his back pocket — crumpled, half-burned — and dropped it on the counter.

No one came to take it.

He lit another cigarette with the stub of the first and stood in the corner, half-hidden by a display of crisps.

Watched the flames on screen.

Watched the fire trucks.

Watched the crowd standing behind the tape, filming with phones, faces full of smoke and curiosity.

But not one of them said his name.

That was the part that stuck.

He was supposed to be dead.

And no one had noticed he wasn't.

The barber shop was closed for good — had been for years.

Kris still had the keys.

He fished them out of his pocket like he didn't expect them to be there. Cold metal. Familiar weight. The third key on the ring stuck in the lock, same as it always did. He jiggled it. It clicked.

The door creaked open on warped hinges. The smell hit him first — old product, dust, sweat dried into leather chairs. Still exactly how he'd left it the night they shut it down after a police raid.

A cracked mirror faced the door.

He didn't look into it.

He flipped the main switch. One strip light came to life overhead — buzzing like it was sick.

The place was a ruin. Empty chairs. Broken clippers. Graffiti in the back room that hadn't been there when he ran the joint. But he knew where the good stuff was — second drawer under the till. Behind the tax folder. Beneath the envelope of old betting slips.

He pulled out the bottle of whisky.

Then a thread spool.

Then a needle.

All things he'd left behind for emergencies. Just never pictured this one.

Kris sat in the middle chair, leaned back, and exhaled.

The shirt came off in pieces — stiff with dried blood and ash. His side was swollen, black-ringed. The cut was wide. Open. Angry. Looked like a shark bite. Or a story he wasn't willing to tell yet.

He cleaned it with whisky and a rag he didn't trust.

He grunted — once — but didn't flinch.

No one else was coming.

No doctor. No stitches. Just him and what he could take.

The needle went in.

His jaw locked.

Thread pulled tight, tearing through his skin like a slow insult.

His breath came in slow bursts. In through the nose. Out through his teeth.

Not once did he curse. Not once did he cry.

Just worked the needle through like he'd done it before. Because he had.

When it was done, he wrapped it with what was left of his shirt. Tied it tight. Drank.

Then sat in silence.

The chair creaked beneath him.

The mirror didn't ask him questions.

The blood slowed.

Outside, the street was still quiet.

But the quiet felt earned now.

The ladder to the roof was still there — rusted, bent at the second rung, but solid.

Kris climbed it barefoot, bottle in hand, stitches pulling at his side with each motion.

No moon tonight.

Just the thick orange haze of streetlights and the low glow of early traffic revving into the new day like it didn't know someone had just died.

The rooftop was wet with dew and city grease.

Black smears of pigeon shit. Old trainers tied to the railing. A half-melted bucket of cement someone had used as an ashtray for years.

Kris stepped to the edge and sat down hard.

Legs dangling.

Bottle uncapped.

The buildings across the road looked pale and unfinished in the low light — windows all blank, curtains not yet opened. The whole city felt like it was pretending to still be asleep.

He drank.

Didn't wince.

Didn't swallow fast or slow. Just enough to dull the edge, but not enough to forget the blade existed.

The stitches tugged again.

He touched them. Still holding.

His palms were lined with blood. Faded now. Streaked across the back of his hand like ink someone had given up trying to scrub away.

Somewhere down the block, a lorry coughed to life.

A door slammed.

Kris didn't move.

He drank again.

Then stood. Wobbled once. Regained his feet.

Held the bottle at shoulder height.

Looked at the street like it owed him something.

Then smashed the bottle against the roof ledge — glass exploded, sharp and bright, catching a little of the morning.

The sound echoed — brief and pointless.

And finally, his voice — raw, quiet, only to himself:

"One down."

Chapter 2 - Funeral for a brother, No Name for the Grave

The earth was wet.

Not freshly dug, just wet — like the ground itself didn't want to hold what was coming.

The casket was unvarnished. Light pine. The kind you'd find in a council catalogue under the phrase "no complications." No handles. No engraving. Just two sets of worn gloves lifting it off the van.

No procession.

No cars.

Just one man with shoulders too thin to carry grief properly. He grunted once as he pulled the weight onto his back and walked it to the hole without speaking.

No priest.

No eulogy.

Just a council worker, bored and yawning, stood off to the side with a clipboard.

Kris stood at the edge of the grave, hands in his coat pockets.

Left hand still swollen. Right side stitched.

He didn't flinch as the box was lowered. Didn't blink when the straps snapped taut and eased it down like they were lowering bricks.

He hadn't slept.

His shirt was clean but untucked.

Boots caked in mud from somewhere else — not here, not today.

His face was unreadable, but his eyes didn't move from the casket once. He didn't look at the others. Three of them. Maybe four. Silent, spread out like they didn't want to admit they were together.

The only sound was wind catching through the dry trees. Plastic flowers rattled somewhere nearby.

No one brought real ones.

Kris watched the coffin hit the bottom with a soft, final thud.

The man with the gloves looked up for instructions.

Kris didn't give any. Just lit a cigarette. Held it with the tips of his fingers like he didn't plan on finishing it.

The gravedigger began to shovel.

Each strike of dirt landed with a sound that was far too quiet for the weight it carried.

Still, no one spoke.

Not even to say Ade's name.

The engine was off, but the air inside the car still hummed — faint static from the old radio that never worked properly, and the low hiss of wind through a cracked window.

Maya sat behind the wheel, coat draped over her lap like a second skin.

One boot resting on the brake pedal. The other foot tapping a rhythm on the floor she didn't know she was keeping.

She could see the grave from here.

Didn't need to be close to know how empty it felt.

The window was open just enough to let the smoke out, but the cigarette in her fingers hadn't been touched in five minutes. Just burned down on its own. A thin trail of ash hung from the end, bent by the breeze and the time it had taken to say nothing.

Kris stood out there like a man propped up for display.

Shoulders squared. Chin down. The kind of stillness that didn't come from peace — but exhaustion.

Maya had seen it before. On soldiers. On killers.

On people who'd survived things they shouldn't have.

He wasn't grieving. Not yet.

Grief had a delay with men like him.

It came later, when you were drunk or trying to shave or teaching a child to tie their shoes — and it would hit you like a punch from behind.

She didn't feel sorry for him.

Not exactly.

But she felt the distance between them widening, inch by inch, with every minute he didn't look up.

The gravedigger was still shovelling. One of the cousins — was it Lek? Or Arben? — lit a cigarette and stood awkwardly near the edge like he wasn't sure if he was allowed to be there.

Maya rolled her own window higher, slowly, until only a sliver of air was left.

She whispered, "Fuck's sake, Ade," but not like a curse.

More like a failed prayer.

Then leaned her head against the glass and watched Kris not move.

They'd expected more people.

Not a crowd — not flowers and speeches and three-piece suits — but a presence. A reminder.

Ade might've been many things, but he was the brother. He was the name. For years, people had walked faster past his shadow.

And now?

A few cousins. One of the old drivers. A man who might've been security, but never spoke.

Nobody looked each other in the eye.

They stood like mourners at the wrong funeral — unsure if they'd shown up to pay respects, or just to check if the man was really dead.

The wind shifted.

Someone coughed.

Kris still hadn't moved.

He didn't need to. He was the reason they hadn't come closer.

Everyone there — the few that dared show — watched him like he might do something sudden.

He didn't.

He just stood there, coat unbuttoned, hands in pockets, cigarette burned down to the filter. Ash clung to his lip and didn't fall.

Behind him, the grave was filling.

One shovel. No rush. No ceremony.

Among the names that were missing:

- Pavli, from the old Romford lot — didn't show.

- Gjin, who owed Ade his life — nowhere.

- Levan's cousin — deliberately absent. Everyone noticed.

- Even Drin — the only other name that should've mattered — hadn't sent a single call.

No one said any of their names out loud, but you could feel them hanging in the spaces between conversation that never started.

Maya, still in the car, lit another cigarette she wouldn't smoke.

The grave got smaller.

The silence didn't.

And Kris, watching it all, blinked for the first time in what felt like hours.

The gravedigger didn't say a word when he finished.

Just stepped back, wiped the shovel on the grass, and nodded toward the clipboard under his arm.

Protocol.

There wasn't going to be a proper headstone. Not yet. Too much heat. Too many questions.

So they gave him a marker — laminated, white, pegged into the dirt like something you'd find on a construction site.

Kris walked toward it alone.

The others stayed back, like the air near the grave was colder.

He stopped in front of the marker and looked down.

"ADAM LEWIS – 1985–2025"

Block capitals. Council font. Something printed, not carved. Not remembered.

Fake name. Fake date of birth. Fake everything.

A man who never existed, buried in a hole like he never did anything worth remembering.

No mention of Ade.

No sign that this was the man who once ran corners from Tottenham to Thamesmead.

No hint that this body had once ordered a dozen men to disappear like smoke.

Kris stared at it.

Said nothing.

Didn't even scowl.

He pulled another cigarette from the box in his coat — last one — and lit it off the glowing ember of the one already in his mouth.

The wind caught the smoke and flung it sideways.

Behind him, Maya's car hadn't moved.

A bird cried out, high and harsh, and was gone before anyone looked up.

Kris exhaled slow. Not angry. Not sad. Just… hollow.

He flicked ash onto the fresh dirt and let it stay there.

Then said, almost too quiet to hear:

"Could've picked a better name."

~Manchester

The pub wasn't even classy.

Stripped walls. Sticky floor. A jukebox that didn't work unless you hit it first. The kind of place no one asked names — just watched how fast you drank and who you came in with.

Drin leaned back in his booth, bottle in one hand, lips too loose.

Three lads around him — not real friends. Just orbit. Faces from the new side hustle he was building up north. Young, too loud, too easy to impress.

He raised the bottle again. Didn't even wait for anyone else.

"To Ade," he said, smiling wide. "May he finally learn how to shut the fuck up."

They laughed — nervously. One coughed. Another lifted his glass halfway, unsure if it was a joke or a trap.

Drin didn't care. He was halfway through the bottle and bleeding swagger.

His phone buzzed. He ignored it.

He tilted the bottle back again, wiped his mouth with the sleeve of a jacket he didn't buy, then leaned forward.

"You know what the problem was?"

He didn't wait.

"He thought fear was the same as respect. It ain't. Respect's what happens when people still say your name after you're gone."

He tapped the table once.

Looked each of them in the eye.

Held it long enough to make them twitch.

"And guess what? They're gonna be saying mine."

The pub door opened. A man in a long coat stepped in. Didn't sit. Didn't smile.

Just watched.

Drin didn't notice.

He was still laughing. Still toasting. Still celebrating a funeral he hadn't attended — a name he hadn't dared say in London.

It wasn't the war itself.

Not yet.

But that night, someone remembered.

And someone reported.

And the fuse, already lit, burned a little closer to the stick.

Chapter 3 - The Boy That Wouldn't Bow

It was supposed to be quiet.

Just a handoff — one case, four envelopes, no drama.

Instead, Drin walked in like he was auditioning for his own legend.

The location was wrong from the start. A car park behind a shopping centre, half-lit, too exposed. CCTV on three angles, and no exit that didn't funnel you past public eyes.

Two Albanian boys waited by a beat-up Lexus, faces drawn, already tense. They were new to Manchester, used to silence and simplicity. Not this.

Drin stepped out of a hired Audi with tinted windows and music still playing — not loud, but deliberate.

He didn't lower the volume.

Didn't kill the engine.

He wore a camel coat over a black tracksuit and sunglasses, even though it was 10:30 at night. Chain heavy. Smile heavier.

Neron and Spence flanked him, both younger, both visibly armed.

One of the Albanians raised a hand halfway — polite gesture, neutral — and said, "You come alone?"

Drin laughed. Big. Wide. Threw his arms out.

"Alone? You're standing in front of a fucking Brutalist, and you ask if I come alone?"

The name dropped like a brick.

Both men stiffened. One glanced toward the CCTV. The other looked past Drin, scanning the shadows like they expected something to move.

Drin didn't notice. Or didn't care.

He stepped forward, pulled open the case — stacks inside, clean-cut, plastic-bound — and shoved it toward them.

"You take this, you deal with us now. No more back channels. No more slow walks. You want work, you come through me. You want war, you see what my family does to cities."

A pause.

Then he added, almost sweet:

"But tonight? We're just making friends."

Phones were already out.

A group of teens across the car park — hooded, hungry, filming the whole thing.

Neron saw them. Nudged Drin.

"Bro, we're live. Let's bounce."

But Drin smiled for the camera.

Held up two fingers. Peace sign. Gang sign. Something in-between. Then tapped his chest twice, right over the chain.

"Long live the Brutalists."

By sunrise, the clip had been reposted fifty times.

A caption added:

"Who the fuck is this?"

And by midday —

Sariah had seen it.

The phone rang twice before he picked up.

"Hello?" Drin answered like he didn't already know who it was.

He was lying on a sofa in his rental flat — half-empty bottle of Cîroc beside him, one trainer still on. Shirtless. Lit only by the pulsing blue of the TV screen, muted.

Maya's voice was clean. Sharp.

"Take the video down."

Drin smirked. Sat up.

"You watching fan edits of me now? Thought you were the classy one."

Silence on the line.

He rubbed his face, leaned back, kicked the coffee table for no reason.

"It's not a big deal. I didn't say anything illegal."

"You said everything stupid," Maya replied. Calm. Measured. "And you used our name to do it."

Drin stood up now, pacing, a little sway in his step.

"Our name? Maya, no offence, yeah, but I don't remember you ever throwing a punch for that name. You think standing in the room while the men made decisions counts as legacy?"

She didn't rise to it.

"You want to play boss, do it on your own time. You start dragging heat onto this family, you won't get a second call. You'll get something else."

Drin scoffed. Walked to the fridge. Nothing inside but a half-eaten takeaway and a single yoghurt.

"You talk like you're still someone. The Brutalists died with Ade. All I'm doing is reminding people we existed."

"No," Maya said. "What you're doing is making us a target. Loud men always die first."

Drin laughed, but it was thinner now. He didn't like how quiet his flat suddenly felt.

"Maybe they do. But at least they get remembered."

Maya didn't answer.

The line clicked. Dead.

He stared at the phone for a long moment, like he expected it to ring again.

It didn't.

And somewhere across the river, Maya reached for her second burner.

And started calling names Drin had never heard.

The warehouse stank of bleach, sweat, and cheap smoke bombs.

Red light buzzed through the rafters like a migraine. A DJ played bass-heavy grime from a setup made of plastic crates and an iPad. The floor vibrated with every drop.

Drin stood on an overturned keg in the centre of it all, arms outstretched, shirt open like he thought it made him look dangerous instead of sweaty.

He wasn't supposed to throw the party.

No one had cleared the space. No permits. No silence.

Just a hundred bodies, sweat-soaked and sideways drunk, bouncing to beats they'd forget by morning.

Drin had ordered everything.

- Tables stacked with pills wrapped in foil.
- Bottles of vodka lined up like trophies.
- Girls flown in from Bristol — hired for atmosphere, not conversation.
- Three of his boys patrolling with visible weapons and no clue what they'd do if someone actually stepped wrong.

He raised a glass.

No mic. Just his voice.

"Tonight's not about money," he shouted.

"It's about names. Legacy. We're not trying to be like them. We are them."

Nobody asked who them was. They just nodded. Drunk. Bored. Waiting for the next track to drop.

"This is the start of something. A reset. They kept it in the dark too long. London boys, whispering in back rooms like ghosts."

He looked around like he expected applause.

Got silence. Then someone cheered, late. One of his own.

"Now we're loud. Now we let the world know."

He lifted a pistol from his waistband — real — held it up.

Not fired. Just flashed. Like a badge he hadn't earned.

A couple of girls shifted uneasily. One of them whispered something to her friend and walked toward the exit.

Drin didn't notice. Or didn't care.

He thought this was what power looked like:

- Red light
- Cheap applause
- And fear that didn't last past the hangover

He took a swig from the bottle and held his arms out again.

"Brutalists don't retire. We take over."

Most nodded.

None of them believed it.

The punch that dropped Neron came out of nowhere.

One swing — solid, square to the jaw — and he was down.

It happened outside the same warehouse, three nights after the party.

Drin was inside with his latest entourage, laughing loud at his own jokes.

Neron had stepped out to take a piss and walked straight into a problem.

Two lads from Oldham. Connected. Different weight class.

They weren't after him. They wanted Drin.

But Neron was in the way.

He didn't run.

Didn't even blink.

Tried to tell them they were barking up the wrong tree.

They didn't care.

They made a point. With fists. With boots. With brass in one hand and a threat in the other.

"Tell your boss to stop putting his name in places it don't belong."

Then they left him bleeding behind the bins.

Nothing broken — except pride, maybe a couple of teeth.

Drin didn't visit the hospital.

Didn't even call.

He sent Spence with a burner and a muttered, "Tell him to rest up. We got plans coming."

Neron didn't say much.

Didn't need to.

The next day, he stopped answering messages.

The day after that, one of the new kids asked, "Who's actually in charge here?"

Too loud. In front of too many.

It was a stupid question — but no one corrected him.

Drin posted a photo that night:

Him, bottle in hand, surrounded by fake gold and real weapons, captioned:

"Legacy don't die. It multiplies."

The likes rolled in.

But the loyalty didn't.

Not everyone said it out loud.

But more than a few had started thinking the same thing:

"If he ain't gonna protect his own… why should we bleed for him?"

The lounge was silent.

No music. Just the soft hum of old wiring and the slow crack of melting ice in untouched glasses.

Maya sat back, coat still on, one leg crossed over the other.

She hadn't touched her drink.

Sariah was already halfway through hers. No makeup. No pretense. Just black jeans, an ash-grey tee, and a stare that could freeze blood midstream.

Across the table, the light flickered.

Didn't matter.

Maya leaned forward, finally speaking:

"He's using the name like a punchline. Flashing it in front of strangers. Throwing parties with weapons out in the open. It's not power — it's suicide."

Sariah didn't respond.

Just reached for the pack of cigarettes beside her, tapped one free, and lit it with a smooth motion that said she'd been doing this long before any of them were worth naming.

Maya went on.

"I warned him. He laughed. He told me I 'never threw a punch.' That he's the legacy now."

She sipped her water. Barely.

"He's dragging us into a war before the first bullet's even fired."

Sariah's eyes didn't move.

She smoked.

Slow. Sharp. Then stubbed the cigarette out in an empty saucer.

She didn't ask for more details. Didn't ask for proof.

Instead, she reached for the napkin beneath her glass.

Pulled a pen from the inside of her jacket.

And wrote a single name:

Drin.

Then slid it to the middle of the table.

No speech. No threat. No ceremony.

Just a name.

Written clean.

Underlined once.

"He's not the future," Sariah said, voice flat. "He's a hole in the boat. And we're already ankle-deep."

Maya nodded.

Said nothing more.

And outside the lounge, the city kept turning —

but the list had just begun.

Chapter 4 - Family Meeting, Fire In The Middle

The café was closed — had been for years — but the back door was still coded, the kind you had to hit twice in the middle before the latch would shift.

No name on the door. No bell. Just a scratched-out buzzer and a faint bloodstain someone never bothered to bleach properly from the handle.

Inside, the air was still thick with grease and burnt coffee. A staircase led up to the private room — what used to be a stock room, now repurposed into what the family called "the table." Not because there was one — but because once you were in that room, you were part of the table. Or beneath it.

Arben was the first to arrive.

He climbed the stairs slow, shoulders square, expression unreadable.

He didn't knock. Just stepped in.

Sariah was already there.

She sat at the end of the long, uneven table — the one Ade had always taken, just right of the old radiator.

She didn't speak. Didn't nod.

She just glanced up once to acknowledge him, then went back to the folder in front of her. Nothing flashy. Just paper, printed. With names.

Next came Lek, then Marjeta, then Jon.

No one spoke much. Just the shuffling of jackets. The sound of chairs pulled half-heartedly from the wall. The nervous tapping of phones that didn't have service in here — reception deliberately blocked since the police raid in 2019.

They looked older than last time.

Or maybe it was just the tension that aged them.

By the time the fifth body entered, the door stayed open too long and let in a draft.

Sariah didn't react.

She sat still, one leg crossed over the other, a cigarette burning untouched in a tray beside her.

No one sat in the seat to her right.

Ade's seat.

The one no one had dared fill — not yet.

When the door opened again, the air changed.

Kris stepped in.

He didn't speak.

Didn't look at anyone.

Just walked the perimeter of the room once, slow, like checking the exits — then stopped in the corner and leaned against the wall, arms folded.

He didn't sit.

The quiet deepened.

No one asked when Drin was arriving.

No one dared ask what would happen when he did.

Kris didn't blink for the first five minutes.

The room kept glancing at him — not directly, but like checking if a power line was still live. No one asked how he was. No one dared. The bruises on his temple were still fresh, and the gauze beneath his coat wasn't subtle.

He leaned against the wall with his arms crossed tight.

Not defensive — just keeping something in.

His stare was heavy. It dragged across the table like a slow hand pulling everything into silence.

Marjeta coughed.

Lek looked at the floor.

Even Arben tapped his leg twice — an old habit from when the police used to sit him in front of mirrors.

Still, Kris didn't move.

Didn't speak.

The chair beside Sariah — Ade's chair — sat untouched.

A bottle of water sweated on the table next to it. No glass.

No name card. Just space.

It didn't matter. Everyone knew what that chair meant. What it used to mean.

And what it didn't anymore.

Sariah hadn't offered it to anyone.

She kept her folder open, flipping a page once with the slow patience of someone who didn't mind being waited on.

Her nails tapped the paper softly.

She didn't look at Kris, but she didn't need to.

They hadn't spoken since the funeral.

He hadn't returned her message.

She hadn't sent another.

But they were both here now — and the space between them felt thinner than the air.

Somewhere outside, a siren whined down the street and faded.

A child shouted in the flat above. A dog barked once, then stopped.

Inside, the family sat in a room where the walls felt closer than before.

No one knew what would be said.

But everyone knew why they were here.

The footsteps up the stairs were too fast.

Wrong rhythm — all bounce, no weight. Drin kicked the door open like he expected applause, then stood in the threshold with both arms raised like he was entering a club, not a family meeting.

"Evening, cousins."

His voice hit the room too sharp.

He was grinning. Hood up. Chain out. Chewing gum like a punchline.

"Hope I didn't miss the buffet."

Nobody laughed.

Well — Jon let out a quiet snort, immediately regretted it.

Drin walked in anyway, clapping his hands once. He didn't nod at Kris. Didn't acknowledge the way everyone's eyes shifted the second he stepped into the light.

He spotted the empty seat next to Sariah — Ade's — and made a slow, deliberate step toward it.

Sariah didn't move.

Didn't blink.

Drin stopped.

Smirked.

"Right. Sacred ground and all that."

He turned, dropped into a creaking chair two seats away, tossed his feet up on another like it was his own kitchen.

"Look, I know emotions are high. I know some of you are feeling a little…" — he waved his hand vaguely — "…sentimental. But come on. A meeting? In a room like this? Over a video?"

No one spoke.

He pulled his phone out, held it up like a trophy.

"It's a good clip. Got reach. Bit of buzz. Don't see the problem."

Kris shifted.

Barely. Just a tilt of the head. Eyes locked now.

Drin saw it. Laughed.

"Kris, you alright? You look like you been dug up, mate."

Silence. Not cold — dead.

Drin's smirk faltered for the first time. He scratched his chin. Still performed.

"Look, I'm just saying. We can't stay invisible forever. Ade kept us in the dark like we were myth. People don't respect ghosts anymore. They respect noise. Reach. Flash."

He looked around the table.

"What, none of you see that? No one's got vision?"

Sariah finally closed the folder in front of her.

Not fast. Not loud. Just precise.

Then she stood up.

Slow. Measured.

And the whole room, including Drin, shut up.

Sariah didn't raise her voice.

She didn't need to.

She stood with both hands resting lightly on the table, her weight balanced evenly, shoulders square. Her gaze never moved from Drin, but her words weren't just for him — they were for the room.

"Three videos," she said. "Three."

No names. No dates.

Everyone knew what she meant.

"One outside a car park with a gun you don't know how to use. One in a flat that got raided forty-eight hours later. And one in a warehouse full of strangers. Where you called yourself a legacy."

She paused.

Drin didn't blink, but he stopped chewing the gum. It stuck to the side of his molar.

Sariah went on.

"Two fights started in your name. One debt made on your word. Five shipments disrupted by your mouth."

She took a breath.

Then stepped toward him — not far. Just enough to let the table know she wasn't talking theory anymore.

"No one asked you to lead. No one asked you to speak. You're standing in front of a history you don't understand with your trousers halfway down and a phone in your hand."

She reached into her coat pocket and slid a photo across the table — low-res still from one of the videos. A face half-visible behind Drin. A known name. A dangerous one.

"Do you know who that is?"

Drin didn't answer.

Sariah didn't wait.

"He's got family in Didsbury. Brothers in Salford. And a father that knows people you've only read about. You flashed your chain and gave them an excuse. That's what you've done. Not legacy — liability."

The room stayed quiet. No one moved.

Then she said it. Plain. Cold.

"If you do it again…"

She stepped back, slowly.

"…I won't be speaking to you next time."

She didn't raise her voice.

Didn't threaten.

Just stated.

Then sat.

And the room, for the first time in years, remembered what real power sounded like.

Chairs scraped back like they were trying not to offend the floor.

No one spoke. No handshakes. No nods. Just slow movements — coats lifted from the backs of chairs, zips drawn halfway, glances exchanged like quiet warnings.

Jon slipped out first.

Then Marjeta.

Then Lek, with a muttered excuse no one asked for.

Even Arben moved like a man who had more to say but knew better than to say it in front of the wrong silence.

Drin sat still a second longer than the others, leaning back in his chair like nothing touched him — except his jaw had clenched. Tight. Tight enough to tremble.

He didn't look at Sariah.

Didn't look at Kris.

He stood, popped his shoulders, and walked to the door with a swagger that didn't reach his eyes.

Just before stepping out, he turned and said — to no one in particular:

"Cool speech."

Then he left.

The door shut behind him too hard.

Kris hadn't moved the entire time. Still in the corner, arms folded, head low.

Sariah didn't look at him.

Not until the room was empty except the two of them.

Then he stepped away from the wall.

Slow. Deliberate. One step. Then another.

He stopped beside her.

Looked down. Studied her face like it might give him something. A signal. A regret. An answer.

She stared back.

Long silence.

Then Kris said, quiet:

"You waited too long."

Sariah held his gaze. Didn't blink.

"I was hoping he'd figure it out."

Kris shook his head once, slow.

"Hope's for people who can afford it."

He turned. Walked out.

And in the alley behind the café, Drin was already on his phone.

"Yeah. Line me up a meet. No Londoners."

A pause.

"Fuck it — make it serious."

And just like that, the storm started moving north again.

Chapter 5 - The First Body That Belonged To Both of Them

The first person to see the body was a boy walking to school.

He dropped his sandwich. Didn't scream. Just ran. Smart kid.

By the time the butcher came out to smoke, the alley was already swarming with tape and blue gloves. A constable was trying not to throw up. Another one took photos like he wasn't sure what angle would make this less real.

Esko lay face-down in the greasewater between a skip and a wall tagged with old turf lines.

His jacket was still zipped, but the back of his head was split open.

His tongue was gone.

Clean cut.

No hesitation.

Whoever did it hadn't just wanted him dead — they wanted the message clear. This wasn't random. It wasn't robbery. It was a statement.

His wallet was gone. His phone smashed under his hand like he'd tried to call someone before it happened. Blood had soaked through his hoodie and pooled under his cheek.

They left his chain.

That was the part that mattered.

The chain was a gift from Ade.

Engraved on the underside:

"Only forward."

The police marked it as gang-related and closed off the alley.

They didn't know who he was.

But the right people did. Within an hour, it reached Maya.

Within two, it reached Kris.

By the time the sun was fully up, the corners had already changed.

People stopped talking.

Stopped walking too slow.

Stopped asking questions.

And over in Hackney, Kris lit a cigarette with shaking hands and said only one thing:

"They picked him on purpose."

By noon, the street had changed its tone.

The shops still opened. The buses still ran. But the pace — the rhythm — it all slowed.

Eyes dropped.

Lips stayed shut.

Everyone knew, but no one said.

At the chicken shop where Esko used to post up, two of the regulars were missing. Not sick — just gone.

Same over at Hoxley's Garage. No deliveries. No music. No banter.

Even the old men who played dominos by the bins had packed up early, their table folded, the cracked white tiles left in a carrier bag under the bench.

The block was mourning — not with tears, but with quiet.

News moved faster than vans.

No texts. Just looks.

A nod at the end of a hallway. A name passed low between door frames.

"It was for them."

"It was that crew from Moss Side."

"Esko ran his mouth."

"Drin dragged the heat in."

"This ain't the end."

You couldn't prove who did it. Not clean.

But the signature was there: the cut, the chain left untouched, the silence after.

That kind of kill wasn't about territory. It was about memory.

And now everyone who'd ever said "Brutalist" out loud was suddenly choosing a side.

Some whispered back to Sariah.

Others started dodging Kris's calls.

A few just disappeared, numbers disconnected, flats abandoned. Ghosts overnight.

And deep in the backroom of a closed kebab shop in Leyton, a kid named Ashif — no more than nineteen — dropped a burner into a bucket of bleach and muttered:

"Fuck this city."

Because the streets were waiting.

Not for peace.

But for the next name.

The betting shop smelled like fried wires and cold piss.

Kris pushed the door open just after three — no disguise, no warning. Hoodie up, boots heavy. No one said a word when he walked in. One old man at the machine didn't even turn around, just slid his card into the slot and kept tapping "Repeat Bet."

Kris didn't look at him.

He saw the man he wanted at the back, hunched over a scratchcard like it was going to spell his future in gold dust.

Leko.

Leko used to run with Esko. They sold together under the Archway line, held keys for northbound stock, used to laugh at the same dumb girls and wear matching fake watches.

Now Esko was dead.

And Leko was hiding in plain sight.

Kris walked straight over and grabbed him by the collar — lifted him clean off the stool and slammed him into the glass divider that separated losers from liars.

The old man looked once. Went back to tapping.

"Name," Kris growled.

Leko stammered something — excuse, apology, deflection — didn't matter.

Kris hit him.

Once. Hard.

Right in the nose.

The crunch echoed down the rows of dead screens and fake odds. Blood hit the counter. Not dramatic — just enough.

"Name," Kris repeated.

Leko gasped through it, coughing into his sleeve. His hands shook. He tried to hold up two fingers but couldn't steady them.

"Man… man from the north, bruv — name's Samo. Heavy set. Bald. Got the accent."

Kris let him drop.

Leko slid down the divider, smearing it with red. Wiped at his nose, tears in his eyes, not from pain — from fear.

Kris crouched beside him, calm now. Cold.

"Next time I ask, you answer quicker."

Then he stood.

Adjusted his coat.

And walked out past the flashing "CLOSED" sign that had never meant anything to anyone until now.

Outside, he lit a cigarette with the same hand he'd just used to break a nose.

And said, under his breath:

"Samo."

Sariah's flat overlooked nothing.

No skyline. No river. No romantic shadows of London architecture. Just rooftops, chimneys, and an estate across the road with more CCTV than balconies.

She didn't invite Kris in.

He came anyway.

She was barefoot, sleeves rolled up, sat at the kitchen table with three phones in front of her. Two active. One stripped.

A single ashtray overflowed in the middle.

Coffee gone cold beside it.

She didn't look up when he walked in.

Just said, "Sit."

He didn't. He stayed standing, back against the fridge, arms folded like iron rebar through his coat.

"I got a name."

She lit a cigarette, nodded once. No surprise.

"I'm guessing you didn't get it gently."

Kris didn't answer.

Didn't need to.

Sariah exhaled slowly, watching the smoke twist through the low kitchen light.

"You don't move yet."

Kris's jaw tensed.

"He was one of ours."

"He was one of Drin's," she corrected. "And that matters."

"Not to me."

"It should."

She finally looked at him — full in the face — and for a second, something passed between them. Not warmth. Not empathy. Something ancestral. Brutalist.

"I've got three people tracing the call logs from Esko's last drop. If we act before we know how they got him, we send a message we might not recover from."

Kris didn't move.

Didn't blink.

"You want quiet," he said. "I want blood."

Sariah stood now. Slow. Calm.

"You want closure. That's not what we do."

He stepped forward, closing the distance, nose to nose.

"You're playing chess with people who play Russian roulette."

Her voice dropped.

"Then let them pull the trigger. When they miss — I'll bury them myself."

Neither one moved.

The flat was silent, except for the low hum of a broken fridge and the ticking of the gas meter behind the wall.

Kris turned. Walked to the door.

Before he opened it, he said:

"When you're ready to do this properly… call me."

He left.

Sariah lit another cigarette.

And stared at the name written on the burner's lock screen: Samo.

It was almost midnight when the knock came.

No rhythm to it — no code. Just five hard raps against the back door of the old Hackney café, like someone didn't care if they woke the dead.

Maya opened it, half-expecting a threat.

Instead, she found a woman in a thick coat and a headscarf, face shadowed, holding nothing but a carrier bag and a folded newspaper.

She didn't ask to come in.

She just said:

"I'm Esko's mother."

Maya stepped back.

Said nothing.

She didn't need to fetch Sariah — the sound of the name alone brought her down the hallway like a wire pulled tight.

Sariah appeared in the doorway behind her.

Bare feet. Hoodie. Silence.

The two women stood face to face.

Esko's mum had no makeup on, no visible grief.

Just lines around her mouth from holding too much in, and fingers that wouldn't stop shaking — not from fear, from restraint.

She didn't ask what happened.

She already knew.

She didn't ask for money.

Didn't ask for names.

Didn't scream, accuse, or collapse into arms that never held her son.

Instead, she asked:

"Who's next?"

Sariah didn't answer.

"Because if it's not going to stop, then someone needs to say. I don't want flowers. I want to know how many funerals I need to prepare for."

The wind moved through the alley behind her, carrying sounds from the road — a siren, a motorbike, a baby crying four houses down.

Sariah stood still, both hands in the front pocket of her hoodie.

Nothing in her posture looked weak.

But her silence spoke louder than anything else in that moment.

After a beat, Esko's mother nodded like she understood something ugly.

Like she knew what Sariah wouldn't say.

"Then I'll light the candle myself. For all of them."

She turned.

Walked back down the steps.

Didn't look back.

Sariah watched until the night swallowed her coat.

Then she closed the door, slowly.

And said, without turning:

"Tell Kris he was right."

Chapter 6 - The Party That Didn't End Well

Same warehouse.

Same playlist.

Same show.

But nothing felt the same.

The air was wrong — thick with the kind of tension that didn't buzz, it dragged. The walls still bled red light, and the bass still hit like a heartbeat out of rhythm. But this time, no one danced near the centre.

They leaned on walls. Scrolled their phones. Smiled too wide and left their coats on.

Drin stood on the balcony above the floor, eyes glazed with something sharp and chemical, grinning like he still owned the night. Behind him, a girl in a mesh dress poured more tequila into his cup and kissed his shoulder like she couldn't wait for the music to stop.

Spence leaned on the rail beside him. Watching. Quiet.

"Feels light," he said.

Drin waved it off.

"It's early. They'll come."

Spence didn't answer.

Because he already knew — they wouldn't.

Word had spread since Esko. About Drin. About his parties. About the heat.

Half the people here tonight were new. Not London boys. Not even Manchester. Just drifters. Clingers. Strangers looking for free smoke and a way to say they were close to something dangerous.

None of the old faces showed.

No Neron. No Ashif.

Even the DJ didn't bother mixing anymore — just tapped through the playlist like a tired algorithm.

Still, Drin moved like it was all fine.

Arms thrown around people's shoulders, dropping names like breadcrumbs, laughing too loud at jokes no one made.

He held court over a room that wasn't listening anymore.

And below, someone in a black tracksuit watched him from the shadows.

Didn't smile.

Didn't blink.

Just sent a short message from a burner.

"It's happening tonight."

Drin grabbed the bottle like it owed him something.

Stumbled forward to the edge of the mezzanine, raised it above his head like a war banner.

His grin was too wide. Teeth too white. Nose flushed pink. Whatever was in his system had already turned his pulse into a drumbeat behind his eyes.

"Listen up, yeah?" he called out, voice cutting through the music like a bottle scraping tile.

"Little announcement from your host for the evening — the future king of this whole fucking game!"

A few heads turned.

Most didn't.

Below, one guy chuckled — nervous, not amused. Another turned to his mate and whispered something that made them both shake their heads. A girl near the bar checked her phone and mouthed, "Let's go soon."

Drin didn't see any of it.

He lifted the bottle higher.

Spilled half of it down his coat.

"They said I'd get us killed," he slurred. "Said I was noise. But guess what — they're not here tonight, are they? They're sittin' in some dead room talkin' rules and fuckin'… family tradition or whatever."

He grinned.

"I got more legacy in my left bollock than—"

Spence was already on him.

Hand on his arm, low voice in his ear.

"Let it go. You've made your point."

Drin laughed him off.

"Nah. Nah, let 'em hear it. They need to remember who started this wave. Me. I did that. I took it off mute."

A beat passed.

Then he raised the bottle again, tried to force a cheer:

"To the new Brutalists!"

No one raised a glass.

No one responded.

A few people turned toward the exits.

Someone else — hoodie up, by the stairwell — was filming.

And across the room, Spence saw it:

- The silence after the noise.
- The stillness.
- The quiet clicks of burners being unlocked under the tables.
- That split-second stillness before a storm.

He touched his waist.

Checked for the piece.

And told himself:

We need to go. Now.

But it was already too late.

The voice didn't cut through the music — it sliced it.

"You think you're Ade?"

It came from below, near the makeshift bar.

Kye. Slouched on a crate, bottle in one hand, jaw tight. His eyes red, clothes twisted like he hadn't slept or hadn't cared to. Maybe both.

People turned.

No one moved.

Drin squinted from above.

"Say again?"

Kye stood now, the wobble in his step not from nerves — from drink. Rage-drunk.

He didn't shout to be heard. He shouted to make it known.

"You ain't him, bruv. You ain't never been him."

Half the room froze.

The other half started drifting sideways, toward shadows, toward exits.

Spence's hand went to his waistband — not drawn, just ready.

Drin leaned forward, smiling too hard.

"You got something you wanna get off your chest, yeah?"

Kye pointed straight up.

"You're gonna get us killed. All your noise, all your big-man speeches — and for what? So some girl can post a clip and say she partied with the 'new face' of London?"

He scoffed. Looked around the room.

"Look around you, bruv. These ain't soldiers. These are tourists. They don't back you. They came for free drinks and a story."

Someone in the back laughed under their breath.

Kye went on.

"You think wearing Ade's chain makes you heavy? You think posting straps on Insta makes you dangerous? You're a fuckin' parody."

Two people had their phones out now. Not hiding it.

One of them texted something short.

A name.

A postcode.

A signal.

Drin stepped back from the rail. His smile was still there, but it twitched now — left corner rising too high.

"Say it again."

Kye didn't.

He just stood still, chest heaving, hand clenching the bottle like he was daring someone to make a move.

Spence looked at Drin and mouthed:

"This ain't the place."

But the place didn't care.

Because downstairs, by the back door, the latch had already lifted.

And someone was inside who wasn't there five seconds ago.

The first thing anyone heard was the slam of the back door.

Not kicked. Shouldered. No warning. Just steel against steel — loud, sudden, final.

The DJ stopped mid-track.

The bass cut off like a power surge.

Then silence.

Then footsteps.

Fast. Heavy. Measured.

Three men in dark jackets moved through the smoke — not shouting, not flashing anything. Just walking straight into the crowd like they'd been here before.

One of them pulled something from his waistband.

Not a blade.

Not a bottle.

Steel.

And that's when it started.

Screams.

Shouts.

A body hitting the crates.

Someone pushed over the speaker tower.

Then came the first gunshot.

Loud. Flat. Echoing.

Not wild — placed.

Then another. Closer.

The warehouse collapsed into chaos.

People ducked, sprinted, dropped bottles, dropped friends. One girl was screaming someone's name — another was pulling her by the wrist, saying "It's not worth it, come on, come on—"

Drin had already hit the floor — not from instinct, from impact. Someone shoved him backwards, elbowed him in the mouth trying to get past.

Blood in his teeth.

Spence was over him in seconds, grabbing the collar of his coat, dragging him behind a stack of crates near the stairwell.

"You see where it came from?" Drin spat.

Spence didn't answer.

Didn't need to.

Another shot rang out — closer this time. Then a yell.

"Kye's hit!" someone screamed.

Too late.

Drin twisted to look — saw Kye stumble once, arms spread like a slow fall. Then collapse, knees buckling underneath him, head smacking tile. A smear of red followed.

People poured out the back door now like floodwater.

Spence didn't let go.

Dragged Drin through the dark, shoulder to shoulder with panicking bodies, heads ducked, shoes slipping.

Outside, tyres screeched.

One of the black jackets vanished into the alley.

Police wouldn't be far now — someone always called when the shots hit close.

Behind them, the warehouse flickered with the last strobe of its fake joy.

And Kye bled out alone on the floor where no one stayed long enough to say his name again.

The call came in just after two.

Sariah was in bed but not sleeping — phone facedown, burner lit, ceiling staring back like it owed her an apology.

She answered on the second ring.

Didn't speak first.

The voice on the other end was shaking. Young. Female.

"It's Maia. I was at the party."

Sariah sat up, slow.

The sheets didn't rustle.

"What happened?"

Maia swallowed audibly. Sirens whined in the background, distant but closing.

"It went off. Shots. Real shots. One guy down. Everyone ran. Drin was gone before anyone hit the ground."

"Who's dead?"

"I think… Kye. I think he didn't make it."

Sariah closed her eyes.

Exhaled through her nose.

"How many shooters?"

"Three. Maybe four. Masks. No colours."

"And Drin?"

"Ran like a bitch."

The silence that followed wasn't empty. It was full — with something heavy and irreversible.

Sariah looked down at her palms, scarred where glass had once bit.

The scars were pale now. But the ache wasn't.

"You did good, Maia."

"You gonna clean it?"

"Yeah."

Click. Call ended.

Sariah sat still for a moment, then stood.

Walked to the table in the corner of the room and unlocked the drawer.

Inside: a burner. A map. A name.

She picked up the burner.

Typed one word.

Sent it to Kris.

"Now."

She didn't say what.

Didn't say who.

Didn't say go.

But he'd been waiting for that word since Ade's lungs stopped moving.

Chapter 7 - The Last Time Drin Was Touched

Enfield, two blocks from the A10.

A tower with nine floors and five working intercoms, where doors stuck, lifts groaned, and the walls stank of whatever takeaway was on special that week.

Flat 6B had a pink door. Painted by someone's daughter.

Drin told her to keep it — "made the place feel less dead."

She'd laughed like it was a compliment.

Now it was midnight. Curtains drawn. TV on low.

Drin sat on the floor with a half-eaten box of chicken next to him, thumb scrolling through burner messages like they held answers.

His nose was still swollen from the stampede at the party. Lip split. He hadn't washed properly. Kept the light off in the bathroom because he couldn't look at his own reflection without seeing Kye's blood.

He didn't know Maya had clocked his postcode the second he ran.

Didn't know a kid in the stairwell had taken a picture of him yesterday with his hood too low.

Didn't know Kris had been sitting in a car three streets over for the past half hour, engine off, phone screen dark, just waiting.

Drin was mumbling something to himself — plans, excuses, half-finished threats — when the girl he was staying with came out of the bedroom, dressing gown on, annoyed.

"You eating on the floor again?"

Drin didn't look up.

"It's cooler down here."

"You look like shit."

"Thanks."

She stepped over his legs, went to the kitchen.

Opened the fridge. Shut it again.

"You want anything?"

He shook his head.

But she was already halfway back to the bedroom when he said it.

Then — a sound.

Not from inside.

From the landing.

Not footsteps. Weight.

One step.

Another.

The girl paused, looked at the door.

"You expecting someone?"

Drin sat up straighter, heartbeat climbing fast.

"No."

The girl moved toward the door, confused.

Her hand touched the lock.

"Don't—" Drin started.

Too late.

The door didn't open.

It shattered inward.

Splinters. Slam. Scream.

And there he was.

Kris.

Boots heavy. Eyes cold.

Not breathing hard. Not blinking.

No words.

Just in.

Drin scrambled backward, palms slipping on the vinyl floor.

"Kris—"

No use.

Kris didn't speak.

He stepped in over the broken door, slow, boots crunching through the busted frame, his shadow swallowing the hallway behind him. His coat was still zipped, but his hands were already bare — fists flexed, knuckles pale.

The girl screamed, backed into the bedroom, slammed the door.

Didn't lock it.

Didn't matter.

Drin got to his feet like a deer — not a fighter — knees bent, neck turned, eyes looking for a way out that didn't exist.

"I didn't mean for Kye—"

Kris moved.

No charge. No shout. Just closed the space between them with three heavy steps and slammed Drin into the fridge so hard the magnets fell off.

Drin gasped. Swung an elbow.

Kris ducked it, grabbed the back of his neck, and threw him sideways into the counter. A pot crashed. Drin hit the floor.

"Please—listen—"

Kris didn't.

He lifted him again — full arm under his ribs — and drove him shoulder-first into the sink.

Crack.

Drin howled.

"You don't—know—what they said to me—!"

Kris dropped him.

Drin collapsed in a heap. Clutching his side. Coughing. Trying to crawl. His hands smeared blood onto the laminate.

Kris didn't follow.

Not yet.

He watched.

Let him move. Let him scrabble like a rat under the light.

"You think I don't know where you've been hiding?" Kris finally said, voice like gravel dragged slow.

"You think Maya didn't know the second you ran from that warehouse like a fucking child?"

Drin whimpered. Didn't respond.

Kris stepped closer.

Lowered to one knee.

"You think this is still your family?"

Drin lifted his head just enough to see Kris's face.

Then the fist came down.

Once.

Twice.

And the room stopped being a flat.

It became a warning.

Six minutes.

That's how long it lasted.

No shouting.

No guns.

Just work.

Kris didn't move like a man in a rage — he moved like a man fulfilling a debt.

Quiet. Mechanical. Every strike with purpose. Every blow measured to damage, not kill.

Drin stopped screaming after the third hit.

His jaw was cracked by the fourth.

He tried to crawl again — Kris dragged him back by the ankle and drove his heel down into the back of Drin's thigh, deep, just above the knee.

Drin's leg spasmed.

Then nothing.

He rolled to his side, coughed blood, and muttered something soft — a name, maybe. A sorry. A prayer.

Kris didn't respond.

He pulled Drin up by the collar, pinned him against the wall by the gas meter, and drove a fist into his stomach so hard the plaster cracked behind him.

Then again.

And again.

Drin's body went limp. But Kris held him up.

Not out of mercy.

Out of clarity.

He wanted him awake. Wanted him present for the ending.

In the hallway, the bedroom door creaked open. The girl stepped out, white-faced, phone shaking in her hand.

Kris turned his head once. Just looked at her.

She bolted.

Didn't scream. Didn't threaten to call the cops.

Just ran.

Down the corridor. Out the pink door.

Gone.

No one on the floor came to check.

No neighbours opened their doors.

The tower had seen worse. And worse had survived.

Back inside, Kris dropped Drin onto the floor like a bin bag.

Drin wheezed. Rolled. Curled.

His right eye was swollen shut. His nose was leaking blood and spit. His hands twitched like they'd forgotten what they were for.

Kris knelt beside him.

Pulled his phone out.

And dialled.

Maya held the phone steady.

One shot. One angle.

No zoom. No edits.

Just a slow pan from left to right — across the floor of the flat, the edge of the smashed table, and finally, to Drin.

He was curled in on himself near the radiator.

One eye purple. One arm bent wrong.

The floor slick under him — blood and something thicker.

He didn't speak.

Didn't whimper.

Didn't even try to move.

The light from the hallway bulb flickered above him like it was unsure whether to stay on.

Kris stood a few feet away.

Boots planted. Hands loose at his sides.

Breathing slow.

He didn't look at the camera until the very end.

When he did, it wasn't rage.

It wasn't pride.

It was cold. Final.

Like a seal being pressed into wax.

"This is what you are now."

Click.

Maya ended the recording.

Thirty-eight seconds.

No context. No date stamp. No ID.

Just truth.

By the time the video hit the burner circuit — passed from one encrypted group to another, from ends to ends, from mouths to murmurs — the only caption it needed was:

"This is what happens when you touch family."

By sunrise, it had been seen over a thousand times.

By breakfast, double that.

Not on TikTok. Not on YouTube. Not anywhere public.

But it moved. Fast.

Telegram groups lit up like crime scenes.

Burners buzzed from Edmonton to Erdington.

And in chicken shops, barbers, and vape dens, kids passed the phone like a holy text:

"That's Drin?"

"Nah — can't be."

"Man looks finished."

"Kris did that."

"You see his eye? Swollen like a fuckin' melon."

"That ain't a warning. That's burial."

The comments started as whispers.

Then came the memes.

Then came the silence.

Because after that? No one stood next to Drin. Not even in pictures.

His name got unfollowed.

His calls got ignored.

His name got left off group chats.

Some even called him by a different name entirely — "The Boy Who Got Touched."

It was the funeral without a coffin.

The death of reputation.

And in this city — that's worse than bleeding out.

In a small flat in Peckham, a girl watched it twice, then muttered to herself:

"He should've died. That would've been cleaner."

But Sariah didn't want clean.

She wanted it loud.

She wanted them to see.

And now, the streets had seen.

Chapter 8 - When The North Comes Back South

The cars didn't belong there.

Too quiet.

Too still.

Too clean for Clapton.

Parked nose-to-tail on a narrow back street off the high road, engines off, windows cracked just enough to hear the city breathing around them. Streetlamp above them flickered like it didn't want to see what was inside.

First car:

An Audi. Blacked out.

Driver heavyset, bald, chain visible even in the dark.

Samo. The one who got named.

Didn't flinch when he did.

Second car:

A battered silver Passat. Smelled like petrol and fake pine.

Passenger seat:

Briggs. Lean. Jumpy fingers. Glasgow accent buried under Manchester vowels. Always smiling for the wrong reasons.

They weren't here for questions.

They were here to finish a sentence.

Between them sat a single folded page.

Four names.

Two crossed off already.

ADE

DRIN

KRIS

SARIAH

Briggs tapped the next one with his knuckle.

"Pub first?"

Samo nodded once.

Didn't speak.

They opened the doors in sync.

No rush. No masks.

Just gloves. And something that clinked when they walked.

Over the roof of the Audi, they bumped fists.

"No shouting," Briggs muttered.

"No hesitation," Samo said.

Then they walked off into the London dark —

north faces, south mission.

And a fire following behind them.

The Whitmore sat tucked beneath a rail bridge — one of those old brick pubs that never closed properly, even when it should have.

Most nights, it reeked of piss, bleach, and yesterday's lager.

Tonight, the shutters were half-down.

Lights dim.

Last two regulars slipping out the side, drunk enough to mistake danger for a cab ride.

Inside, the barback was mopping.

Toothpick in his mouth. Headphones on.

Samo pushed the door open with one hand.

Didn't announce himself.

Behind him, Briggs leaned against the wall outside, one eye on the street, hand inside his coat where glass clinked.

The mop stopped moving.

The barback turned, squinting.

"We're closed, bruv."

Samo didn't reply.

He didn't have to.

Because that's when the bottle came.

Through the air, tight and clean.

Briggs's arm arched from the pavement like a striker taking a free kick.

It hit the far corner of the bar.

Glass shattered. Liquid kissed flame.

Boom.

A pulse of orange exploded across the counter, caught the rag bin, and jumped to the wall like it knew the layout.

The barback screamed — not from pain, from shock.

Too fast. Too hot. Too sudden.

Within ten seconds, the kitchen door lit up like a matchbook.

The fire didn't spread. It consumed.

Briggs slipped the second bottle back in his coat.

Didn't need it.

Inside, the last thing Samo said before turning back to the door was:

"Tell her we're not waiting anymore."

Then he was gone.

Flames cracked the window behind him.

The Whitmore burned silently — no sirens yet, no neighbours watching —

just smoke rising into the London dark,

and a war kicking its boots off.

The second stop was colder.

Not emotionally. Physically. The wind by then had teeth, and the high-rise flats near Stamford Hill caught every bit of it.

Briggs pulled his hood tight. Samo didn't blink. His jaw looked carved from something prehistoric.

Flat 22 sat halfway up the block — but they weren't going inside. They didn't need to.

They knew what it held: a deadbolt, two safes, one cracked-wall bedroom that doubled as a ledger room.

No straps.

No crew.

Just a brain.

Kris's kind of spot. Clean, tucked, vital.

Which is why it had to burn.

They lit the rag in silence — no showboating, no chanting.

Just the quiet woof of a flame catching thick cloth, and the controlled step as Briggs leaned in and fed it to the base of the door.

Paint came next.

Thick, sloppy.

The can hissed as Samo moved like he'd done this too many times before.

Not art — just declaration.

He finished it with one hard line under the words and stepped back.

YOU STARTED IT

Big. Red. Across the bricks like blood made to dry in public.

As they walked off, Briggs didn't smile. He lit a cigarette. Tossed the match behind him.

The fire was small, but deliberate — just enough to bite into the frame, chew up the seal, blacken the outer wall.

Not an inferno.

A warning.

By the time it was spotted, they were already back in the Audi.

Doors shut. Engine on.

Samo looked at the passenger seat, where the folded paper still sat.

Kris and Sariah.

Both unchecked.

Briggs flicked ash out the window.

"Next week?"

Samo nodded.

By the time Kris arrived, the fire was out — mostly.

The building hadn't been evacuated. The city was too used to smoke.

Residents leaned on balconies above, hooded, watching without speaking. Someone's aunt muttered something in Yoruba and went back inside. A kid in sliders filmed a TikTok with the burning smell still clinging to the bricks.

Kris didn't look up at any of them.

He parked, cut the engine, and walked across the courtyard alone.

The wind carried soot. The last wisps of smoke curled from the scorched doorframe of Flat 22 like fingers retreating into shadow.

There was no siren now. No flames.

Just the after.

The red spray-paint across the wall had started to run in the damp:

YOU STARTED IT

The drips made it look like the wall was bleeding.

Kris crouched low by the steps and picked something up:

a half-melted burner phone. Its screen cracked.

Still warm.

He turned it over in his palm, slow.

And in the faint reflection of the dark glass, his face stared back.

No expression.

No flinch.

Not even surprise.

Just that look.

The one people whispered about.

The one Spence said he hadn't seen since Ade.

Kris stood. Pocketed the phone.

Didn't call anyone.

Didn't need to.

Because fire had been thrown.

Which meant fire was owed.

The room was dark except for the table light.

No windows. No distractions. Just the map.

It was the old paper kind — taped flat across the centre of the table, the edges yellowing at the folds. London splayed out like a body on an operating table. Every borough marked. Every shortcut and backdoor alley pencilled in from memory.

Sariah stood in a tracksuit and vest, barefoot, two coins in her hand.

One landed on Hackney.

The other — a little south — just between Stamford Hill and Finsbury Park.

"Pub," she muttered. Clink.

"Flat." Clink.

Kris stood to her left, jaw locked, eyes heavy.

He hadn't said a word since he walked in.

On the far edge of the table sat an envelope. Thick. Unsealed.

Inside: names.

Turncoats.

Fence-sitters.

London boys who were now answering phones from the North.

Sariah opened it, skimmed the top five, then laid it flat beside the map.

"They're not looking to provoke. They're looking to burn."

She moved her hand over the river, tapped twice on Southwark.

"They hit us once, we hit back harder. That's how it used to be."

Kris finally spoke.

"Used to be, they didn't cross the M25."

Sariah didn't smile.

She didn't even look at him.

She picked up a black marker, circled both coin spots, then wrote two letters beside each:

R

E

"Retaliate. Eliminate."

Kris nodded once.

Sariah still didn't look up when she said:

"No more improvising. No one gets touched unless I say so. From now on — it's planned. Understood?"

Kris said nothing.

Just walked to the door.

Right before stepping out, he said:

"Then say the word. Sooner."

And the door clicked shut behind him.

Chapter 9 - Spence Gets In The Way

The bench wasn't special.

Not hidden. Not famous. Just old. The kind with rusted screws, warped slats, and chipped blue paint from a council project no one funded twice.

Spence sat there with his hood up and a burner balanced on his thigh.

It was 3:07 a.m.

Nothing good ever happens at 3:07 a.m.

Around him: silence, broken only by wind brushing through plastic bags caught in the railings. A single streetlamp buzzed overhead, lighting the corner of the park where dealers used to post up before CCTV moved them three blocks east.

Spence didn't come here for nostalgia.

He came here because Dino said he'd meet him.

Dino wasn't one of theirs anymore — not for a long time.

He'd flipped north. Worked small ends under the Manchester umbrella now.

But he owed Spence.

A ride. A debt. A favour that once saved his ribs from getting stove'd in behind a gym in Walthamstow.

Spence thought it might mean something.

He was wrong.

But right now, he didn't know that yet.

He lit a cigarette with fingers that wouldn't stop twitching.

Not fear. Just doubt.

This was the first time in weeks he'd moved outside the house without Sariah knowing.

He hadn't told Kris either.

Didn't want the look. The silence.

Didn't want to hear "Leave it."

Because Spence wasn't built like them.

He didn't get high off revenge.

He didn't dream about fire.

He just wanted a pause. Long enough to breathe. Long enough for someone — anyone — to remember that even wolves used to eat at the same table.

He took a drag. Exhaled. Looked down at the phone.

One unread message from Dino:

"Come alone."

He typed:

"I did."

Sent.

Then he waited.

Twenty minutes.

That's how long it took for everything to go sideways.

Stonebridge at night didn't feel like London.

It felt like some in-between place — a holding cell between now and never, where time dragged and the wind never came from one direction.

Spence walked slow. Hands in his coat. Hood up.

No weapon. Just the burner and a pack of nicotine gum.

Stupid.

The alley behind the estate ran between two bins and the back of a kebab shop.

It stank of bleach, oil, and piss.

He stood in the middle, lit only by the strip light mounted above a metal fire door. The bulb buzzed like a warning.

Then he heard it — not boots. Trainers. Scuffing the grit behind the bin.

He turned just as Dino stepped out.

Taller than before. Heavier. Wearing black.

Didn't wave. Didn't nod. Just walked until there were five feet between them.

Spence didn't smile.

"Thanks for coming."

Dino sniffed. Looked over his shoulder once. Too casual.

"I'm not here for long. Say what you need."

Spence took a step forward. Measured.

"This thing between the families—if it carries on, everyone loses. You know that. Even your side."

Dino tilted his head, mock-thoughtful.

"Yeah?"

"You ain't got the bodies to hold London. No one does. Not now."

Silence.

Dino shifted on his feet.

"You always thought too much," he muttered.

Spence's brow twitched. His gut turned.

He took half a step back.

"Who else is here?"

That's when the figure moved — from behind the bins, face covered, quick. Not big. Not loud. But fast.

Spence turned to run, but too late — the shove caught him across the shoulder.

He stumbled. Reached for balance.

Bang.

A shot — tight and low.

Close range. Muffled.

His leg went.

It didn't feel like pain at first. Just wrong.

Like his body didn't believe it had been hit.

He collapsed sideways, mouth open, no sound.

Dirt in his teeth. Blood through denim.

Dino said nothing.

Didn't even stay to watch.

Just pulled the hoodie back up and vanished into the black like nothing had happened.

Spence stared at the sky.

Then the alley.

Then nothing.

Maya was supposed to be asleep.

But something about how Spence left — no goodbye, no jacket zipped all the way, no keys in his usual pocket — made her sit up in bed.

And follow.

She stayed two blocks behind, walking like she had somewhere else to be.

Hood low. Headphones in.

No music playing.

When he turned toward Stonebridge, she stopped pretending.

Twenty minutes later, she was crouched behind the same bins he didn't see coming from.

By the time the shot rang out, she was already moving.

Spence didn't scream.

Didn't even twitch when she reached him.

His face was chalk-white. Eyes flickering.

Breathing shallow, like his body couldn't decide whether it wanted to keep trying.

She dropped to her knees beside him, grabbed his cheeks.

"Hey. Hey. Look at me."

He didn't.

"You're not dying in this fuckin' alley. You hear me?"

Nothing.

She patted down his coat, found the burner, shoved it in her waistband.

Then she moved. Fast.

No 999. No ambulance.

Just a minicab — flagged with a frantic wave on a corner three streets over.

The driver saw the blood and nearly kept going.

Maya stepped in front of the car like a brick wall.

"He got clipped on a bike. Look, please. Just get us to Royal London."

"I don't—"

"I'll give you three bills. Cash."

He unlocked the doors.

Back seat.

Spence was semi-conscious now, mumbling something broken, fingers twitching against her thigh.

Maya pressed his head into her lap, used her coat to hold pressure on the leg.

"You're not going anywhere," she whispered.

And for the first time, Spence looked at her — really looked — like she was the only real thing left in the world.

Then his eyes rolled back.

The cab kept moving.

And Maya didn't cry.

Didn't panic.

She just held his head and stared out the window like she was already writing names.

Hospital lights didn't hum — they buzzed. Loud and steady like a bad omen.

Spence woke to that sound, eyelids sticky, throat raw, body weightless on one side and burning on the other.

His leg was wrapped tight. IV in one arm. Heart monitor blinked like an impatient warning.

No flowers.

No card.

No Maya.

Just silence.

The morphine kept things soft around the edges, but the pain still found him — a dull, stabbing kind of hurt, the kind that made you want to laugh just to prove your teeth were still there.

It wasn't until the second night that someone came.

Not Kris.

Not Maya.

A man in a grey overcoat with prison tattoos visible up to his neck. Built like an old bouncer, walked like he still bounced.

He stood at the foot of the bed, checked the vitals, then reached into his coat and pulled out a folded slip of paper.

Read from it.

"You acted without the house."

He looked up. No emotion. No edge. Just statement.

"That makes you vulnerable."

Spence didn't respond.

The man let the silence hang.

"There's no punishment. Yet. But this ain't gonna be forgotten."

He dropped the paper on the side table, turned, and walked out.

Didn't check if Spence was breathing.

Didn't care.

Outside, Sariah was waiting — not in the car, not pacing. Just standing in the rain under a broken streetlight with her arms crossed.

She never went up.

Didn't ask for an update.

She already knew what mattered:

He lived.

Which meant he could think about what he'd done.

The door opened just after 2 a.m.

No footsteps. No knock. Just the soft click of cheap hinges and the scent of cold wind that came in with him.

Kris.

Still in black. Still wearing the same jacket from the fire. His face unreadable, pale from the streetlight, eyes heavy like they hadn't closed since the attack.

He didn't say anything when he walked in.

Didn't ask how Spence was.

Didn't sit down.

Just stood at the foot of the bed and looked at him like he was trying to find a shape in something that used to be solid.

Spence blinked slowly. His mouth dry.

"Kris…"

The name came out thin. Almost embarrassed.

Kris didn't respond.

Seconds passed.

Then minutes.

Then finally, quietly:

"Don't do that again."

It wasn't loud.

It wasn't angry.

But it cut.

And Spence heard what was underneath it — the weight behind the line, the distance in it. Like Kris was already packing the grief in advance. Like he couldn't do it a second time.

Spence opened his mouth to speak, maybe explain, maybe beg—

But Kris had already turned.

He walked out with the same silence he brought in.

No hand on the door.

No backward glance.

Just gone.

And in the beep of the heart monitor and the ache in his ribs, Spence understood:

That was it.

Chapter 10 - What You Start, You Finish

The door to the backroom was already open when Kris walked in.

No knock. No ask. Just footsteps and silence.

Sariah was sitting at the small square table by the far wall, teacup in front of her, full but untouched. Steam had stopped rising from it. Her fingers tapped slow against the ceramic.

On the table:

A burner.

A folded receipt.

A single black glove.

Kris didn't sit.

Sariah didn't look up at first. She just spoke.

"Stonebridge was his doing. The alley. The shot."

Kris said nothing.

"He used your boy to make a point."

Still no response.

Then she looked at him — not long. Just enough.

"You finish it."

She pushed the burner across the table. Kris picked it up.

Screen lit. Address on the screen.

MILLBANK ESTATE, FLAT 12C — TUESDAY NIGHT DROP. DINO.

Kris slid the phone into his pocket.

"You don't want a body on this side," he said, not as a question.

Sariah nodded. One deliberate motion.

"No mess. No attention. You know how to make a man disappear without the sirens."

Kris cracked a knuckle. Rolled his neck. Still didn't sit.

"I won't bring him back."

She leaned back in the chair. Picked up the cold tea. Didn't drink it.

"Good."

That was it.

No further instructions.

No good lucks.

No warnings.

Just the weight of the green light —

quiet, official, permanent.

Kris turned and left without another word.

Behind him, the glove still sat on the table, untouched.

The car was old. Not untraceable — just forgettable.

Black Vauxhall Astra with a cracked aux port and enough cigarette burns in the fabric to suggest four previous lives.

Kris drove it like he didn't plan to bring it back.

No music.

No podcast.

Just the engine, the road, and his own mind chewing itself raw.

It was past 2 a.m.

M25 empty.

The signs overhead all fluorescent lies — "Think. Don't Drink." "Keep Your Distance."

Kris wasn't drinking.

And anyone close tonight wasn't staying conscious long.

He passed Watford like it didn't exist.

Didn't look at the phone again — didn't need the address. It was already carved behind his eyes.

Millbank Estate. Flat 12C.

Tuesday drop.

Dino.

He didn't bring a blade.

Didn't bring a strap.

Didn't bring gloves.

Just a black hoodie, a burner with Maya's number in it, and one sentence that kept pulsing behind his teeth like a bad heartbeat:

You used my brother.

That wasn't strategy.

That was debt.

And Dino was overdue.

He stopped for petrol once — didn't speak to the cashier. Paid cash. Didn't blink when she asked if he wanted a receipt.

"No."

The drive took just under three hours.

By the time he hit the edge of the estate, the streetlights had all gone to sleep and the sky had that bruised-purple look, like it had seen too much and didn't want to watch anymore.

Kris parked.

Stepped out.

And zipped his hoodie slowly, like it was armour.

Then he started walking.

Not toward the stairs.

Not toward the lifts.

Toward the noise — low voices, cheap laughs, and the unmistakable echo of someone who thought they were safe.

The estate was halfway built, halfway condemned — one of those concrete skeletons meant to be luxury flats until someone pulled funding and the rats moved in faster than the realtors.

Dino was on the third floor.

Sat on the ledge of an unfinished balcony with two other boys and a speaker pumping drill that'd already died twice.

He was laughing at something stupid — probably his own joke.

Didn't see Kris step through the gap in the scaffolding.

Didn't clock the figure moving up the back stairs until it was too late.

Kris came up the wrong way on purpose — no echo.

His boots didn't even creak.

By the time Dino noticed, the other boys had already moved — that sixth-sense twitch of the smart ones, the ones who know when the air shifts.

"Yo—Kris? What the—"

Kris didn't answer.

He just stepped forward, grabbed Dino by the front of his North Face and slammed him back into the stairwell wall. One of the other runners flinched — then ran.

The second hesitated.

Kris turned just enough to meet his eyes.

"Go."

The kid vanished.

Dino tried to speak.

"Wait—wait, listen—I didn't mean for—"

Crack.

Kris's fist collided with Dino's knee — a clean shot, straight down. The sound it made echoed off the concrete like a snapped branch in a tunnel.

Dino howled.

Kris grabbed the other leg — drove it sideways into the wall.

Another break.

No rage.

No breathing hard.

Just method.

Dino collapsed, halfway seated, knees bent wrong, palms raised like surrender might work.

"Kris, please—I'm not the one who pulled the—"

Kris grabbed him by the jaw, thumb inside the cheek, and squeezed.

"You lined him up."

"It wasn't personal, man—"

Crack.

His jaw shifted sideways.

Something tore.

He screamed — a noise like a child who knew he'd done something unforgivable.

Then Kris moved lower. Took Dino's left hand. Pressed it to the concrete.

"You send a message with this hand?"

Dino choked out a sob.

Kris lifted his elbow — and dropped it.

First finger snapped.

Then another.

Then the rest.

One by one.

Dino passed out on the fourth.

Kris let the hand go, wiped the blood off on Dino's jacket, and stood over the mess he'd made.

Still breathing.

Still twitching.

But not walking. Not talking.

And never lining anyone up again.

Kris didn't check for a pulse.

Didn't need to.

He knew Dino was still alive — barely — and that was the point.

Blood was everywhere. Not arterial, but enough to make the floor sticky and the air sharp.

The smashed hand was curled against his chest like it still believed it worked. His jaw sat at a wrong angle, mouth open like he was trying to scream through fog.

Kris didn't look at the face.

He turned the body sideways, slid him down against the wall — knees broken, legs folding in on themselves. Arms slack at his sides. Chin on his chest.

He looked like a discarded warning.

Then Kris reached into his own pocket.

Pulled out a silver pack of Nicorette gum — the same kind Spence always carried. Popped it once in his hand. Looked at it. Placed it carefully inside Dino's coat pocket.

Just enough sticking out that someone would notice it when they searched him later.

Not for Dino.

For Spence.

Kris wiped his hands on the inside hem of his hoodie.

Stood.

No photo.

No proof.

The estate was silent again. The other runners wouldn't come back. Not yet. They'd wait for sunrise, or police tape, whichever arrived first.

As Kris stepped down the stairs, he passed a cracked mirror nailed to the far stairwell wall. He didn't look at it.

He didn't need to see his own face to know what was there.

The flat was quiet.

The kind of quiet that only lives between 5:00 and 6:00 a.m., where even the city feels hungover.

Kris unlocked the door with his elbow.

His hands were still drying.

No one was in the hallway. No light in the kitchen. But the smell of bergamot lingered in the air — sharp, floral, bitter.

Sariah was at the table. Same spot. Same cold tea.

She hadn't slept.

She didn't look up when he stepped in.

Just stirred the cup once with a spoon that had no business being there — slow, delicate, pointless.

Kris said nothing.

He dropped the burner on the counter.

Unzipped the hoodie.

Sat down across from her, blood dried to the cuffs in jagged brown flecks.

She noticed.

She didn't flinch.

She nodded once. Barely a movement.

Then — just before the silence could slip back into something tense — her lips curled.

Not wide.

Not warm.

But real.

A smile.

The first.

"Was it clean?" she asked, not really needing the answer.

Kris looked past her — out the window at the block across the estate, where the light had just clicked on in a flat four stories up.

"It's done."

Sariah picked up the tea. Sipped it cold.

"Good."

And that was it.

Nothing else needed saying.

Because they both knew — when Dino's boys found him, when they saw what was left, when they checked his pocket and found a nicotine packet that didn't belong to him—

They'd know.

This wasn't retaliation.

It was response.

Sariah stood. Walked out.

The door didn't close behind her.

Kris sat alone. Didn't move.

And for the first time since the war started…

He felt tired.

Chapter 11 - The Rules Get Re-Written

It started with silence.

No more bodies on pavements.

No bricks through windows.

No Molotovs tucked in backpacks.

Just… gaps.

Deliveries didn't show.

Product got rerouted.

Money disappeared between Southwark and Croydon like the streets had swallowed it whole.

At first, it looked like coincidence.

Then — coordination.

The North had stopped throwing punches. They started doing surgery.

Inside men. Turned workers.

Boys from Brixton and Bow who'd been on Sariah's payroll for years — now slipping burner locations to Manchester numbers.

A runner got picked up, only to be dropped by officers with no questions asked.

Another stash flat was raided, but nothing was taken — except the drop book.

Someone was trading intel for oxygen.

And it worked.

The house started bleeding — not fast. But constantly.

A kilo here.

A contact gone there.

A burner wiped clean after one too many "accidental" forwards.

Sariah didn't shout.

Didn't kick in doors.

She just started writing names.

With a red pen.

Kris didn't flinch when he saw the list.

But everyone else did.

Because if the North was making soft cuts, Sariah was sharpening something harder.

And when it came down —

it wouldn't be subtle.

The room used to be a spare bedroom.

Now it was a war board.

Walls stripped bare. A cork grid stretched floor to ceiling, plastered with names, mugshots, burner numbers, CCTV stills. Red string weaved from one pin to another — a messy web if you didn't know how to read it.

Sariah knew exactly what it said.

She stood barefoot in joggers and a men's t-shirt. Cold cup of coffee in one hand. Red pen in the other.

A name at the edge of the map — Connor Malik — got a long, steady look. She followed the string from his photo to a side note on a torn envelope:

Sister in Chorlton. Car lease paid in cash.

Sariah took a breath. Crossed him out. One slash, hard enough to dent the wall behind it.

Another name: Denzel Ward.

Circled once.

Then again.

The pen dug in deep enough to leave a red ring around her fingertip.

By the time she stepped back, five names had been altered.

Two erased.

Three marked.

She dropped the pen in a mug by the wall. Took a final sip of coffee, winced at the taste, then turned to the sideboard where an old Nokia burner sat blinking red.

She pressed one key. Let it ring once.

That was enough.

Across London, five lieutenants' phones lit up with the same message:

"Warehouse. 2 a.m. Bring no one. No metal. No lies."

It was the first time since Ade's death that she'd called them all in.

And this time, they wouldn't be leaving with reassurances.

The warehouse was dead quiet.

No signage. No cameras.

Just corrugated steel and the stink of rain off concrete.

It sat behind an old scrapyard in Bermondsey — one of those places that didn't show up on GPS unless you already knew it existed. No one spoke about it.

Everyone showed up anyway.

Inside, a single bulb swung overhead like an interrogation light.

A folding table sat in the centre.

No chairs. No refreshments.

Just space — for decisions.

Six men stood spaced around the edge of the room. All Brutalist affiliates. Some old. Some younger. All had guns in their cars, but none brought them inside.

You don't bring a blade to the butcher's table.

Sariah walked in at 2:03 a.m. sharp.

Kris behind her, black coat, no expression.

She set the briefcase on the table.

Unlatched it. Opened it slow.

Inside:

A stack of contracts.

Each one blank except for a name at the top, and a line at the bottom where the ink didn't dry unless it was mixed with blood.

Sariah didn't look up.

"Things are changing."

Silence.

"We've lost product. We've lost routes. We've lost people."

One man — Hoss from Newham — started to speak.

Kris cut him off with a look.

He stopped.

Sariah stepped away from the table, let the contracts sit exposed under the bulb like a final offer.

"From tonight, the old rules are gone."

She raised her hand and counted them off:

"One. No more third-party drops. You clear a bag, it comes through the house."

"Two. If you get touched by the North and don't speak, you disappear."

"Three. You lie to the table — you die."

Not a single voice responded.

"These papers don't leave the room. You either sign — or you walk now, and don't come back."

Someone shifted their weight.

Someone else scratched a beard.

No one moved.

Sariah nodded once.

"Good."

And behind her, Kris closed the case again.

Like a judge folding the verdict.

Nobody moved when the case shut.

The contracts had been passed, hands blooded, names signed. Not one man argued.

But not everyone had come to sign.

Some had come to answer.

Sariah didn't raise her voice when she read the names.

"Reece Lawson."

A sharp inhale near the back.

"Jerome Kyte."

Jerome flinched like a kid called to the front of the class. Reece stared straight ahead, frozen like he could outlast the air pressure.

Kris stepped forward from the shadows.

"Come."

Not shouted.

Not optional.

Jerome opened his mouth.

"I didn't—"

Kris looked at him.

Jerome stopped speaking.

The two men walked toward the far shuttered exit like they were headed to a smoke break.

No one followed.

No one watched.

The door clicked shut behind them.

Thirty seconds later:

Pop.

A pause.

Pop.

Clean.

Small calibre. No echo.

Then silence again.

Kris returned alone.

Closed the shutter behind him.

Sariah didn't glance at him. Didn't acknowledge the absence of two men.

She turned to the others.

"That's the last time I call names."

She picked up the empty briefcase.

"From now on, you call your own."

And walked out.

They left one at a time.

No handshakes. No nods. No whispered side deals.

Just boots on concrete, slow and steady, as the lieutenants filed out of the warehouse like survivors of a sermon no one had expected to hear.

A few lingered by their cars, eyes flicking to where Kris had walked Reece and Jerome only minutes earlier. But no one asked where the bodies were.

They already knew.

And there was no point asking when your own name might be next.

Inside, the folding table was still there.

The light still swung.

And the briefcase was gone.

Kris was the last one out.

He didn't rush.

Didn't look over his shoulder.

Just turned off the bulb with one long reach, leaving the warehouse in absolute dark, and stepped into the cold morning air like a man walking out of a job he never applied for.

He didn't speak during the drive home.

Didn't light a cigarette.

Didn't even blink when the light drizzle started and stuck to the inside of the windscreen like tears on glass.

His hands stayed locked at ten and two on the wheel.

Knuckles white. Jaw clenched.

Not angry. Not sad.

Ready.

Because what happened tonight wasn't a threat.

It was a shift.

And everyone — every rat, runner, or wrong name — could feel it in their ribs now.

The game wasn't about territory anymore. It was about survival.

Chapter 12 - The Ghost Of Drin

The call came at 4:11 a.m.

Sariah let it ring twice, answered on speaker.

She didn't say hello.

The voice on the other end did.

Slow. Measured. Mancunian.

"Tell Drin he's got twenty-four hours to pay up or someone in your family gets zipped."

No shouting. No threats.

Just the sound of someone who knew he'd been robbed.

"He quoted six," the man continued. "Shifted eleven. Lied about the markup. Took the product. Vanished. That's not a mistake. That's an insult."

Click.

Sariah didn't move.

Didn't even blink.

The room was cold and empty except for the burner on the floor and the weight behind the words.

Drin had made a play — a stupid one.

He bought big, skimmed bigger, and didn't pay back.

It wasn't greed.

It was ego.

He thought being a Brutalist meant immunity.

He was wrong.

By 8:00 a.m., the North had made it public.

Two of their own walked into a gym Sariah's crew ran out of Brixton, cracked a dealer's nose, and said:

"This is what happens when you trust liars."

By noon, someone tagged a butchered pig with the word "THIEF" in red paint and dropped it outside a stash flat in Hackney.

Sariah stood on the second floor of the flat, watching from behind the blinds as two boys tried to clean it up with bin liners and weak stomachs.

She didn't speak.

Kris arrived five minutes later.

Saw the pig.

Didn't ask questions.

Just lit a smoke and said:

"He's going to get us all killed."

She nodded.

One time.

Then picked up the phone.

Pressed 4.

"Family meeting. Tonight."

And hung up.

The meeting was held in the same basement Ade used to use for birthday drinks and death threats.

Low ceiling. Dusty chairs. Muffled traffic overhead like the city was trying to listen in.

There were seven of them in the room.

Only family.

Sariah stood, back straight, arms folded.

Kris sat in the corner, one boot tapping slow against the leg of a plastic chair.

Drin swaggered in late.

No apology.

Still chewing gum, still dressed like he owned air.

"What?" he said, before anyone opened their mouth. "It's not that deep."

No one laughed.

Sariah didn't blink.

Spence leaned against the far wall, arms crossed, expression unreadable. Maya beside him, jaw clenched tight enough to crack a molar.

Drin paced.

"This is business. It's always been business. You act like I robbed a fuckin' church. We've done worse."

Kris looked up.

"You lied."

"So?" Drin snapped. "You think that crew up north wouldn't've pulled the same? We beat 'em to it. I outplayed them."

"You stole from them," Maya shot back. "You didn't even pay for what you asked for. You lied to them and us."

Drin pointed at her.

"You ain't blood."

Spence took a step forward.

"Say that again."

Drin sneered.

"She's not family. She doesn't get a fuckin' vote."

Kris stood.

"You think this is about voting? You put all our names in the dirt. You didn't just rob some mug with a burner — you robbed a supplier who bankrolls whole wars. You don't come back from that with words."

"Then what, huh?" Drin spun. "You gonna kill me, Kris? You gonna bury your own cousin for flipping a few keys?"

Sariah's voice finally cut in.

Cold. Steady. Final.

"No."

The room went silent.

She walked to the door. Paused.

"I will."

And left.

Drin opened his mouth to speak again —

but this time, no one was listening.

The car ride was quiet.

Drin had his feet up on the dash, scrolling something on his phone.

Didn't ask where they were going. Didn't care.

Sariah drove like she was heading to the shop. Left turn, then another. Windows down. The smell of dust and cold metal creeping in.

By the time they reached the construction site — half-finished flats, gutted rooms, wire mesh hanging like ribs from concrete bones — Drin finally looked up.

"What is this? A scare job?"

She killed the engine.

Didn't answer.

He snorted.

"You think this is gonna fix the mess? A bit of show-and-tell? You brought me out here to make me dig or cry or beg or what?"

Sariah got out.

Opened the boot.

Drin followed, slower now, confusion turning into that vague itch of dread.

She didn't bring a spade.

Just a bag. Heavy. Canvas.

He laughed, half-nervous.

"What, you gonna rough me up, yeah? Bit dramatic, Sair."

She opened the bag.

Pulled out a .38 revolver wrapped in butcher paper.

Drin stopped talking.

"You're serious?"

She looked at him.

No hate. No sadness.

Just calculation.

"You endangered the house."

"Come on—"

"You lied to me."

"I was fixing it—"

"You made yourself the boss, Drin. Only problem is, you were never meant to lead."

He took a step back, hand raised. No fire in him now — just sweat and disbelief.

"You wouldn't."

Sariah didn't flinch.

"I already have."

She raised the gun.

Mid-sentence, mid-breath, mid-stupid look—

CRACK.

The shot echoed through the shell of the building like it had been waiting for it. Drin folded backward into the dust. One clean hole above the eye. Eyes open.

Sariah stood still for six seconds.

Then moved.

She dragged the body to the far end of the site where the ground had already been half-torn up by diggers.

It wasn't deep. But deep enough.

She didn't call anyone.

Didn't cover her tracks.

She just dug.

And when the last of him was covered, she stood over the spot and lit a cigarette with dirt still under her nails.

Didn't speak.

Didn't cry.

Just watched the sun start to rise behind the skeleton of a half-built flat.

The sun was barely up when the messages started flying.

"You seen Drin?"

"He's not picking up."

"Last seen in a motor with Sariah."

"Something's wrong."

By noon, the silence had congealed into fact.

Drin was gone.

No post.

No story.

No burner activity.

Just… absence.

At the Brixton flat, Kris was already in the kitchen when Sariah walked in, skin pale, hair still wet from a sink rinse. She made no effort to look rested.

Spence arrived half an hour later. Maya with him.

No one spoke right away.

Then Sariah did.

She didn't wait for a question.

"He's not coming back."

No gasps.

No outbursts.

Just stillness.

"He endangered all of us," she continued. "Put the house in a war we didn't ask for. He did it for ego, and he did it without us."

Spence stared at the floor.

Maya's arms were folded, but her expression didn't change.

Sariah didn't raise her voice.

"I did what needed doing."

Someone on the crew couch coughed. No one acknowledged it.

Kris stepped forward, pulled a chair out, didn't sit. Just stood by her side and said it clearly:

"We back her."

That was it.

Not loyalty.

Not warmth.

Just structure.

Spence looked up — slowly.

"Where's the body?"

Sariah didn't blink.

"Where it belongs."

Spence said nothing. Didn't nod. Didn't argue. Just looked away again.

Two members of the outer crews — Taz from Norwood and Devin from Romford — left the flat without a word. Packed their shit later that night. Gone by dawn.

And nobody chased them.

By the end of the week, no one called it a family anymore.

The word disappeared — slowly at first, then all at once.

Conversations shifted.

No more "we."

Just "Sariah's lot."

"The woman at the top."

"That house."

Because that's what it had become —

A house.

A structure.

Not a home.

Drin's absence wasn't filled.

It was paved over.

Sariah drew up new percentages. No more handshake splits. Everything written, calculated, logged.

Each area had a name. A price. A margin.

No one got more because they were old school.

No one got grace because they were blood.

Loyalty didn't earn rewards now.

Just permission to remain.

The top men were reclassified: no longer brothers, cousins, or "the boys."

They were units.

Blocks.

Operations.

And Sariah watched it all from the top floor like a chess master watching pieces forget they used to bleed.

Kris adapted.

Spence didn't.

He went quieter, colder.

Didn't argue.

Didn't rebel.

Just watched.

And Maya?

She kept her head down. But she didn't smile anymore.

That winter, a new phrase started circulating in the smaller circles, whispered low but always with weight:

"It's Sariah's house now."

And no one — no one — said it like a compliment.

Chapter 13 - Spence Makes A Move

The shoebox was taped shut with electrical wire and a piece of cloth that still smelled faintly like car smoke and black pepper — Ade's aftershave and the ashtray in his old motor.

Spence found it under the floorboards in the spare room, wedged between a ripped bag of 9mm shells and a broken photo frame.

He didn't touch the shells.

Didn't look at the photo.

He opened the box.

Inside:

Three burners.

Two notebooks.

And a slip of till receipt that just said:

"IF I GO, FIND MURPHY."

The handwriting was unmistakable.

Spence sat on the floor, legs folded, and powered up the oldest burner first.

Dead.

Second one buzzed to life — blue backlight flickering, screen cracked.

Contacts: 23.

Only three still had full names.

He tried the first.

Disconnected.

Second.

"This number has been—"

Third:

"Hello?"

Spence didn't speak at first. Just listened. Male voice. Older. Sharp edge, smoker's rasp. Cautious.

"Who's this?"

Spence cleared his throat.

"You knew Ade."

A pause.

"Who's asking?"

"Spence. His cousin."

Another pause — longer this time. Then:

"…You sound like him."

"He left me your name."

The line went silent again, then a cough.

"Jesus. You know what kind of risk this is?"

"Yeah."

"Then why you calling?"

Spence glanced at the note. Thought about the house now — cold, clockwork, full of ghosts and rules that didn't bleed anymore.

"Because I don't like what we became."

The voice sighed.

"Where?"

Spence gave him a location:

Edmonton Green. The old Turkish café near the station.

No cameras. No questions.

"Half an hour," Murphy said.

The line went dead.

Spence sat for a moment longer, phone still in hand, staring at that scrap of receipt.

Then he got up, grabbed his coat, and walked out the flat like he was late for something that mattered.

The café was mostly windows and tired curtains.

A radio played low behind the counter — some late-night Turkish folk song that didn't care who was listening. The place smelled of cardamom, old oil, and chairs that had outlived two owners.

Spence got there first.

He ordered tea, black. Didn't touch it.

Ten minutes passed before Murphy walked in.

Older. Thick grey beard. One eye cloudy from a scar that looked like it had come from something sharp and deserved. He wore a flat cap and a bomber jacket zipped up to the throat.

He looked like someone who used to be somebody.

Spence nodded once.

Murphy sat down.

Didn't order.

Didn't smile.

"You don't look like a leader," Murphy said.

Spence raised a brow.

"That's why I'm here."

Murphy leaned back in the chair, glanced around. No one else was in the place but the bored man behind the counter scrolling through his phone.

"Back then," Murphy said, "Ade walked into a room and you knew something changed. He didn't shout. Didn't have to. People followed because they wanted to. Not because they were afraid."

Spence looked down into his tea. Steam was gone. Flavour too, probably.

"And now?"

Murphy didn't hesitate.

"Now it's a brand. Nothing but cut-throat accounting. You think Sariah's keeping it alive? Nah. She's just putting it on life support with rules and blood."

Spence tapped the side of his cup.

"You walked away."

"Because I knew how it'd end."

"And now?"

Murphy studied him for a long time.

"You're trying to build something. Quietly. Not stupid. Not soft either. But you're doing it without telling her."

Spence didn't answer that.

He didn't have to.

Murphy nodded to himself.

"You find the others?"

Spence slid a folded napkin across the table. Six names.

Murphy's was top.

"I remember."

Murphy looked at the list, then back at Spence.

"Two of these won't talk to you."

"They already have."

That surprised him. Only for a second.

He reached for the napkin, then didn't.

Left it there.

"You really think you can change it?"

Spence gave the first honest answer of the day.

"I think it's worth trying before we all drown."

Murphy let that sit. Then stood.

"You've got my number. Use it once."

He walked out without shaking hands.

Spence didn't finish the tea.

He folded the napkin back up and put it in his coat pocket.

Didn't need to check the names again.

He had them now — and he wasn't letting go.

The living room smelled like weed and antiseptic.

Old spliff rolled on the table. A half-bottle of antiseptic Kris had been dabbing onto a cut above his knuckle — still red, not stitched.

He sat on the arm of the sofa, leg bouncing. Didn't look up as Spence walked in.

Didn't need to.

"You met with Murphy."

Spence closed the door. Quiet.

"Yeah."

Kris didn't speak right away.

Just scratched the scar on his jaw, like it itched when things got wrong.

"You tell her?"

"No."

Kris stood. Walked once around the coffee table. Didn't pace, didn't shout. Just… moved.

"She knows."

Spence nodded. Already figured.

Kris stepped closer. Close enough the space between them felt like an ultimatum waiting to be picked.

"Are you starting something?"

Spence's mouth twitched — not a smile. Just a twitch.

"No."

Kris tilted his head.

"Then what the fuck is this?"

"I'm remembering."

That stopped Kris for a second.

Not because it made sense.

Because it did.

He took a breath, stepped back.

"You think this ends with tea and talks? You think Murphy's boys are gonna walk back in here and fix what got smashed when Ade died?"

"No."

"Then what?"

"Then we stop pretending this is still a family."

Kris looked at him for a long time — really looked.

Then turned.

"She won't forgive this."

"I'm not asking her to."

Kris picked up the antiseptic. Didn't use it. Just held it.

"Careful, Spence."

"Always."

Kris moved to the door. Paused. Without turning around:

"Just make sure you're still in the house when she locks the next one behind her."

Then he left.

Spence didn't move.

Didn't flinch.

He just pulled the napkin from his pocket and stared at the six names again.

Four down.

Two to go.

Sariah said nothing.

Not a word.

Not when she passed Spence on the stairs.

Not when he stepped into the back room for the Tuesday sit-down.

Not even when he spoke directly to her —

"I've got eyes on the Norwood lot, they're twitchy."

— and she looked past him like the wall was more deserving.

Maya noticed. Of course.

She didn't say anything either — but her eyes flicked toward him every time Sariah ignored another comment, another nod, another unspoken request for acknowledgment.

Kris kept his mouth shut.

The crew watched and learned: if Sariah didn't speak to Spence, then Spence didn't exist.

She'd weaponised absence.

She didn't yell. Didn't exile.

She erased.

Spence didn't argue.

Didn't plead.

Didn't even seem to care.

He still turned up. Still took his corner of the room. Still made suggestions — not for approval, not to stir. Just to say them out loud.

He looked different now.

Not broken.

Not defiant.

Clear.

He walked with his hands in his coat pockets and his shoulders low.

A man moving like wind couldn't knock him over anymore.

The more she iced him out, the more deliberate he became.

He didn't raise his voice.

He didn't challenge hers.

He just kept showing up.

And in a place where most men shouted to be noticed, Spence's silence started sounding louder than anything in the room.

The names weren't written anywhere official.

No SIMs. No texts.

Just six on a napkin. Folded once, then again.

Spence took it out one last time.

Two were done — conversations he'd ended himself. One man too old. One woman too bitter.

Four remained.

He'd seen all four.

Not at the same time. Not even in the same week.

One in a car park behind a shuttered bookies.

Another at a funeral.

The third inside a broken lift that didn't move but still hummed like it wanted to.

The last — at a barber shop that didn't cut hair anymore.

Each one gave him something different.

A warning.

A number.

A map.

A promise.

None of them wanted power.

None of them wanted revenge.

What they wanted was structure again.

Not spreadsheets.

Not control.

Not Sariah's brand of order.

Just something that made people feel part of it again.

Spence sat in the back garden of a derelict semi in Tottenham — nothing but bricks, burnt chairs, and silence. Lit a match. Watched the napkin curl.

It burned fast. Quiet.

He didn't need it anymore.

He'd memorised the names.

The voices.

The weight they carried.

He wasn't building a coup.

He was building a shape.

Not a rebellion.

Not yet.

But when it came…

He'd already know who stood where.

Chapter 14 - The Calm Before Nothing

No one fired a shot in six weeks.

No bodies in skips.

No cars torched.

No stash houses breached.

The silence should've been mercy.

It felt like a trick.

Phones still buzzed. Only quieter. Names shared in code, locations whispered instead of typed. If a call lasted more than twenty seconds, people cut the line and changed chips.

The Manchester lot had stopped hitting.

But not because they'd lost.

They were waiting.

And everyone in London could feel it.

Sariah sat at the head of the table — not a table, really, just a repurposed pool table in a boarded-up club off Holloway Road — and listened to the crews speak in tight, anxious bursts.

"Our Camden link's gone quiet."

"Half the Peckham runners want hazard pay."

"Two girls walked from the Dalston lot. Said they ain't dyin' for a postcode."

No arguments.

No shouting.

Just tension.

Like the room itself didn't want to exhale.

Spence stood by the back wall, arms folded. Said nothing.

Kris wasn't there.

That made people more nervous than anything.

One of the younger boys, Rico, cleared his throat.

"This mean we won?"

Sariah looked up — slow, measured.

"You ever win a war where no one says it's over?"

Rico shrank.

Maya leaned in, elbows on the felt.

"Then what are they waiting for?"

Sariah's reply came low.

"A mistake."

The room fell still.

Because they all knew the truth:

Wars don't end with silence.

They just shift into strategy.

And the only question now was which move would cost the most.

The first time he hit someone unprovoked, it was in a pub in Bow.

A man glanced his way — too long, maybe, or maybe not.

Didn't matter.

Kris smashed a glass on the edge of the bar and buried the jagged edge into the man's cheek without warning.

The guy never even got his hands up.

No warning. No words.

Just red.

The next day, it was a kebab shop.

Two teenagers mouthing off at each other.

Kris walked in, heard something — the words didn't matter — and threw one of them through the front window. No one called the police. No one stayed to finish their food.

By the end of the week, he was drinking every night.

Not sociably.

Not even around people.

Just bottle after bottle in his flat with the curtains drawn, chain-smoking in his boxers and punching the walls when his thoughts got too loud.

He didn't even bother hiding it.

Kris showed up to the crew meeting high on something sharper than weed, sniffing, jittery. Shirt untucked. A bruise on his knuckles, fresh and glistening.

Spence clocked it immediately.

"You alright?"

Kris didn't answer. Just stared past him, eyes glassy.

That night, Kris followed a boy through the back streets of Brixton. The kid couldn't have been older than nineteen. No connection. No warning. Just a glance in a pub toilet mirror — a flash of recognition, maybe. Or paranoia.

The alley was silent when Kris stabbed him.

Three times.

No shouting. No mess.

The kid slumped into a crate of flattened cardboard.

Kris walked off without checking his pulse.

The next morning, Maya mentioned hearing something.

Kris didn't blink.

Just said:

"People get lost all the time."

Later that week, a cleaner found the body.

The boy had no priors.

No affiliations.

Just… bad luck.

Sariah heard the news.

Read the name.

Didn't flinch.

Didn't ask questions.

She just lit a cigarette.

And said nothing.

Spence didn't make noise.

While Kris was breaking pint glasses and faces, while Sariah stared through rooms like every voice bored her, Spence moved softer — slower.

Corners of pubs. Back seats of minicabs. Rooftops that hadn't hosted product in years.

Old ground, revisited.

Old names, remembered.

He wasn't asking for soldiers.

He was checking for memory.

Did they remember Ade's time?

Did they remember when being in the house meant more than silence and surviving?

He brought cigarettes. Cheap whisky. No offers.

Just:

"You good?"

"Still working?"

"Still trust what's left?"

Some said no.

More said nothing.

But a few nodded.

That's all he needed.

One night he sat outside a disused barber's in Southall, tapping a burner against his knee. He'd left it on a table inside a week ago — blank SIM, no contacts.

It rang once.

Then stopped.

Two hours later, he got a knock on his flat door.

An envelope pushed under it.

Inside: a photo.

It was of a man Spence hadn't seen since before Ade's funeral.

He didn't smile.

Just folded the photo and slid it into the jacket pocket he rarely wore anymore.

Later, Maya caught him at the flat. Asked how he was sleeping.

"Like a man making maps in the dark."

She didn't press.

She just nodded and left him to it.

Spence lit a roll-up by the window and watched the street below where no one walked with purpose anymore.

He wasn't building an army.

He was counting the ones who remembered the anthem.

The first time she rewound the footage, she told herself it was just a habit.

Security check.

Spence entering through the back stairs of the Brixton flat. Nothing strange about it — coat on, head down, not looking at the camera.

Still, she watched it again.

Slower.

Frame by frame.

He didn't linger on the landing. Didn't speak to anyone.

Didn't do anything that could be called wrong.

But it felt too clean.

Sariah didn't bring it up.

Not with Kris. Not with Maya.

She just took note.

A day later, she checked the ledger.

Spence's cuts were smaller than they used to be — because he'd asked. Said he didn't need as much. Said to push more upstream to the younger crews.

That alone should've been suspicious.

But he hadn't framed it as noble.

Hadn't even explained it.

He just did it.

Too quiet. Too smooth.

Another evening, she walked past him in the kitchen.

He nodded.

She didn't.

Then doubled back five minutes later, just to see if he'd stayed in the same room.

He hadn't.

She didn't ask where he'd gone.

Didn't need to.

He was laying bricks.

And she could feel the outline of a house she hadn't drafted.

One of the runners — a lad called Jakey — mentioned something offhand at a sit-down.

"Spence was in Norwood last night."

Sariah didn't react.

But later, she pulled up the tracker logs.

Spence had borrowed a car registered to a shut-down lockup in Plaistow.

Clean.

Untraceable unless you were looking for it.

Which she now was.

The pieces were lining up, but the picture still felt just out of focus.

Sariah didn't speak on it.

Not yet.

Because sometimes the best way to catch movement…

…was to pretend you were still sleeping.

The mechanic was new.

Young. Too polite.

Didn't know when to lie yet.

"You asked me to do a sweep," he said. "You didn't say what you were expecting."

Sariah didn't look up.

Just lit a cigarette by the garage entrance and nodded once.

The car was on the lift.

Benz C-Class. Armoured. Mint. Supposed to be untraceable.

The boy pointed underneath.

"It's tucked behind the axle casing. Industrial-grade adhesive. Battery's got a lifespan of three weeks, and it's been logging for nine days straight."

"Who else has seen it?"

He blinked.

"No one. Just me. I— I didn't touch it."

"Good."

She stepped forward, bent down, and saw it — the thing no one was supposed to get their hands on.

Small. Sleek. Not some street tracker you buy online for eighty quid and tape with duct.

This was military tier.

Encrypted. Clean.

The kind of thing you plant on a target.

Not a friend.

Not a partner.

A threat.

She stood, exhaled slow, smoke curling under the garage lights.

"Take it out. Leave it in a bin. Pick somewhere random. Tell no one."

"Yes, ma'am."

She walked to the front of the car and placed her palm flat on the bonnet.

Nine days.

That meant someone in the circle.

Someone with access.

Someone who knew when she was alone, and when she wasn't.

This wasn't the start of a war.

This was the warm-up to an execution.

She didn't call Kris.

Didn't call Maya.

Didn't even think about Spence — not yet.

Sariah just stood there, her hand on the car, and started rewalking the last nine days in her head.

Not to remember who she'd trusted.

But to count how many people she'd spared.

Chapter 15 - Static On The Line

The car looked like a ghost.

Gunmetal grey, smudged panels, a bent aerial that hadn't picked up radio since 2017. Still smelled like tobacco and leather. Still ran like sin.

Kris threw himself into the driver's seat and thumped the dash.

"Still got heart."

Spence stood by the iron gate, one brow cocked.

"That thing's a fossil."

Kris grinned.

"Fossils survive wars."

He lit a cigarette with one hand, turned the engine over with the other. The Benz growled alive — old muscle, all sound.

Sariah came out second. Jacket over one shoulder, folder tucked under her arm.

She didn't walk fast.

Didn't speak.

She just eyed the car like it had already betrayed her.

"Why this one?"

Kris jerked a thumb toward the backseat.

"No GPS. No trace. She's a ghost like Ade. Plus it's nostalgia, right?"

Sariah didn't smile. Didn't even blink.

"Nostalgia gets you killed."

He smirked, unlocked the doors with a rusty clunk.

"So does standing still."

She got in. Slow. Settled into the passenger seat without another word.

Spence stayed on the pavement. Arms crossed, face flat.

"You sure you want to roll all in one car?"

Kris flicked ash out the window.

"What, you worried? That the crew might miss our cheekbones?"

"It's not smart."

"Neither are we."

The joke didn't land.

Spence stepped back, let them roll out through the gate. The Benz coughed twice, then smoothed into second like it had never stopped running.

He watched it disappear down the road, that old grey silhouette like something pulled out of a memory he didn't ask for.

Three of them, in one vehicle.

Like it was ten years ago.

Like nothing could touch them.

That was the problem.

Something already had.

The car rolled to a stop outside the old tannery near King's Cross — nothing but shuttered brick, chain-link fences, and sky that threatened rain but didn't bother delivering.

Kris killed the engine and cracked his neck.

"Give me ten minutes. Just gonna have a word with Trey. If he's late again, I'll knock his front teeth into even numbers."

Sariah stayed still, staring at the dashboard clock.

Spence in the back, phone in hand, scrolling but not reading.

Then Sariah's burner buzzed.

Not her main.

Not the crew line.

The one she kept duct-taped to the back of a drawer.

She pulled it out.

UNKNOWN CALLING

00:00:00

She answered. Didn't speak.

The voice on the other end came like gravel and smoke —

digitised, distorted, but familiar in rhythm.

"Get out of the car."

She narrowed her eyes.

Didn't respond.

"You've got five minutes."

"Who is this?"

"Get. Out. Now."

The line went dead.

She stared at the phone.

Kris leaned forward.

"What's that face?"

She looked out the window — nobody around. No vans. No movement. Just the wet-glass quiet of an old street forgotten by traffic.

"Someone just rang. Told me to get out the car."

Kris scoffed.

"Someone?"

"Modulated voice. No ID."

"That's a prank."

"That's money. It was scrambled. Professional."

Spence leaned forward from the back seat, voice low.

"They say how long?"

"Five minutes."

Kris laughed again, but this time there was a ripple under it. Not amusement. Something closer to fear pretending to be cool.

"You lot are joking."

Sariah wasn't.

She unbuckled.

"We're leaving."

"No, we're not. This is a wind-up. Probably that little prick Mace trying to throw us."

Spence had already opened his door.

"It's not a wind-up."

"It's a game, man."

Sariah turned to Kris, eyes sharp.

"So's chess. You still die in it."

She was already out.

Kris hesitated.

Spence wasn't waiting.

He stepped onto the pavement, scanning rooftops, corners, bins. His hand brushed the grip of the pistol inside his jacket. No wind. No watchers.

Kris sighed hard through his nose.

Then, finally, he opened his door.

Too late.

The door hadn't even clicked shut when the world came apart.

BOOM.

A deep, low-body detonation — the kind that doesn't sound like a bang but like a collapse.

The shockwave punched the street.

The Benz lifted, twisted, and split — metal screaming mid-air, wheels thrown like teeth.

Spence hit the ground hard. His ears didn't hear the fall — only a ring, high and constant.

Sariah was tossed backwards, her coat catching fire as she rolled, screaming through clenched teeth.

The car — or what was left of it — crashed back to earth in two halves.

The front was gone.

The back door still hung open, frame twitching.

A chorus of alarms burst to life down the block.

Windows shattered.

Dust and flame belched from the crater, and something wet slapped across the curb where Kris had stood seconds earlier.

Spence crawled toward the smoke, one hand dragging his knee behind him, eyes streaming.

He could taste copper and plastic in his mouth.

Someone — a stranger, a runner maybe — dragged Sariah back from the heat. Her lips were moving, but nothing made it out.

From the wreck, a scream.

Not human. Not full. Just… noise.

Instinct.

A leg.

A shoulder.

Someone still alive in there.

Then — sirens.

One after the other.

Unmarked.

Marked.

Fire and ambulance. No time to check whose jurisdiction it was.

Two firefighters dove in. Didn't even wait for the fire to stop licking the roof.

They dragged someone out — blood-matted hair, shirt scorched black. Barely breathing.

Then another body — limp, still hot, what was left of a coat and a burnt hand.

Zipped.

The zip echoed louder than the blast had.

Sariah watched from the ground, teeth clenched, knees burned through fabric.

Couldn't stand yet.

Didn't know which body was Kris.

Didn't know which one had been pulled out breathing.

She tried to speak.

Nothing came.

Only smoke.

Spence stood in the wreckage smoke, blinking through ash and flashing blue.

The paramedics were already loading one stretcher into the back of the ambulance — oxygen mask over a blackened face, veins collapsed, chest rising in jagged stutters. Still breathing. Barely.

The other?

Zipped.

Unmoving.

Steam coming off the bag.

One firefighter came over. Irish. Mid-thirties. Sweat and soot in his eyes.

"You family?"

Spence just nodded.

"One made it to the back. They're en route to St. George's now. Can't ID. Burn damage. The other's gone."

"Gone?"

The man gestured behind him, toward the black bag lying beneath a tarp. Someone had tried to shield it from the gawkers and the press already rolling up with long lenses.

"Instant. Took the front of the blast."

Spence's throat locked. His jaw clenched so tight his teeth ached.

He tried to say a name.

Nothing came out.

Not Kris.

Not Ade.

Just static in his mouth and iron in his stomach.

Sariah was sitting against a wall now, a silver trauma blanket draped over her shoulders.

Someone had given her a bottle of water.

She hadn't touched it.

Her eyes were locked on the body bag.

But her face didn't crack. Not yet.

Maya arrived seconds later. Hair pinned up. Still in boots.

She walked straight to Spence.

"Who?"

Spence shook his head once, barely moving.

"They won't say."

"You saw who went in the ambulance?"

"Couldn't tell."

She didn't push. Didn't speak again.

They both looked back at the two vehicles — the ambulance doors closing on one life, the tarp hiding the end of another.

No name.

No ID.

No closure.

Just a family split in two.

And only time would tell which half still had breath in it.

It was two hours past the blast when Maya got the burner unlocked.

They were back in the safe flat — the one with no Wi-Fi, no electricity upstairs, and only one way in or out. Windows covered with black cloth. No one spoke.

Sariah sat in the corner with her leg bandaged and one eye bloodshot from the smoke.

Didn't ask how the search was going.

Didn't say a name.

Spence leaned over Maya's shoulder.

She held the SIM between her thumb and forefinger like it might still burn her.

Slotted it in.

Booted the phone.

It buzzed twice.

Then lit up.

Call history: one number.

She clicked into it.

No name.

Just raw digits, longer than standard.

The location trace started populating.

Spence read as it built itself in sections:

Tower 1: Greenwich.

Tower 2: Camden.

Tower 3: Shoreditch.

VPN reroute. Spoofed timestamp.

Signal bounce: internal.

His throat went tight.

Maya looked up.

"This was someone in the house."

Spence didn't speak.

She clicked into the final data log.

One message.

Not a text.

Just a voice snippet.

The same scrambled, hollow distortion that Sariah had heard in the car.

She played it.

"This was the last warning."

Click.

Static.

Then nothing.

Sariah still hadn't moved.

Still hadn't asked.

Still hadn't cried.

She didn't have to.

Someone inside had tried to wipe one of them off the map.

And whoever survived that car bomb — whichever one it was — would wake up into a war that had already begun.

Chapter 16 - The Breathing Half

St. George's Trauma Wing didn't sleep, but the hallway outside Room 213 was unnaturally quiet.

Lights dimmed.

No visitors loitering.

No nurses chatting.

Just one private security guard with a cauliflower ear and a laminated badge that didn't list his real name.

Inside the room, the patient lay still.

Bandaged from chin to brow.

Burns to the chest and arms.

Multiple fractures.

Respiration shallow.

Stable, but unknown.

Not to the staff — they knew the name on the ID tag.

But the name wasn't spoken.

Not to the media.

Not to the cleaners.

Not to the techs adjusting wires and drip lines.

The chart read simply:

BRUTALIST – HOLD

Maya had made the call herself. Two, actually.

The first was to a woman at the Department of Health she'd paid favours to five years earlier.

The second was to a man who could scrub digital records like they were grease off a plate.

Within thirty minutes, the press release was pulled.

No patient matching that age, gender, or injury description existed.

No car bomb ever reached triage.

The only people who knew someone had survived were inside the house.

And none of them were speaking.

At the nurse's station, a file sat half-filled: progress stable, no verbal response, no eye movement yet.

Just one small detail marked in pen under "Visitors":

FAMILY – CLEARED

The nurse who wrote it didn't ask for a name.

She'd been told not to.

And when the visitor came, they didn't announce themselves.

Just flashed a card.

Nodded once.

Walked in, no expression.

The breathing inside the room never changed.

But something in the air did.

Like the future had entered quietly.

And was deciding who to become.

Nobody said the name.

But everyone was saying something.

By morning, the crew house buzzed like a beehive with no queen.

Kris.

Ade.

Kris.

Ade.

Burnt alive.

Still breathing.

Gone.

Not gone.

Every theory carried weight.

And every whisper grew sharper.

"I heard it was Kris — they said the body was tall."

"Nah, it was Ade in the front. Kris got dragged out."

"No one gets dragged out of fire like that and lives."

"It's a message."

"It's a mutiny."

"It's a reckoning."

By noon, two of the lieutenants — Faheem and Sol — packed up and left. Quietly. No goodbye, no threats. Just stripped their burners, left them on the table, and walked out.

Faheem paused at the door long enough to say:

"I ain't dying for a ghost."

The others didn't argue.

That afternoon, someone tried to access Sariah's locked cabinet in the safe room — the one only she and Maya had the codes for. The keypad was scratched. The top hinge loosened. Like someone thought they could pry truth from steel.

Sariah found it.

Didn't mention it.

Just changed the lock.

Replaced the keypad.

Added a second deadbolt.

When Maya asked what she wanted to do about it, Sariah just said:

"They're not ready for the answer."

That night, the house sat in silence.

TV off.

Phones down.

Nobody laughed.

Nobody drank.

Not out of respect.

Out of uncertainty.

Because the person in the hospital bed — whoever they were — would wake up into a kingdom already split.

And if it was Kris…

He wouldn't forgive the disloyalty.

And if it was Ade…

He wouldn't forget the silence.

The power vacuum wasn't official.

No announcement.

No hierarchy shift.

No claim to the throne.

But things still needed doing.

And Maya did them.

The first morning after the explosion, she showed up in a navy coat, bun tight, folder under one arm.

Twelve unread messages.

Four missed calls.

Two burner phones ringing on and off all night.

She didn't return any of them.

Instead, she walked into the back office and started moving numbers.

The Southall safehouse — emptied.

The Bow lock-up — doubled security.

The gear in Stratford? Cleared out. Sent to Brighton under a shell van in under six hours.

She moved cash into clean lines.

Burned every name from the last manifest and started a new one with aliases no one but her would recognise.

By 3 p.m., the Peckham crew were back on rotation.

The Camden girls had new drop sites.

One runner with a big mouth got sent to Manchester on "business."

Everyone called it efficiency.

But it was control.

She didn't bark orders.

Didn't threaten.

She just gave short instructions, never twice, and moved on. If they didn't listen, they got skipped the next day. If they did, they stayed fed.

No one asked who was in charge.

Not when Sariah stayed silent.

Not when Spence disappeared.

Not when the fire was still fresh on the road.

Maya didn't fill the gap.

She simply refused to leave it empty.

And no one — not even the old heads — wanted to test what would happen if they tried to pull it from her hands.

Not yet.

He was there at midnight.

Gone by four.

No one saw Spence leave. No one heard a car. No one checked the door until the morning, when his jacket was missing from the hook and his pillow hadn't moved.

His burner stayed behind.

So did his knife.

No word. No warning.

Just absence.

Maya noticed first. She didn't panic — just ran through a checklist in her head and re-routed two meetings he was supposed to sit in on.

Sariah didn't ask. Didn't even look up when Maya mentioned it.

"He'll come back if he wants to."

He did.

Exactly thirty-two hours later.

The front door cracked open just after dawn, soft, like it might apologise. His silhouette filled the frame — no swagger, no explanation.

His coat was soaked through. Rain, maybe.

Or something worse.

His boots left dark prints behind him, and he didn't make eye contact with anyone as he passed through the hallway. Maya followed.

"Where were you?"

"Out."

"You're bleeding."

"Not mine."

She grabbed his sleeve — gently — and saw his knuckles: skin split, swollen, the edge of a zip-tie burn wrapped around the base of his wrist.

"You went to find something."

"I found it."

He pulled a burner from his coat pocket. Cheap, grey, scratched screen. Still powered.

He didn't hand it to her. Just set it on the kitchen counter beside the tea canister and walked away.

"Wipe it. Read it. Burn it."

"Whose is it?"

He paused at the door. Looked over his shoulder.

"The person who warned Sariah."

Then he was gone again. Upstairs this time. No more answers.

Maya stared at the burner.

Didn't move.

Outside, the first siren of the morning broke the silence.

2:11 a.m.

The hospital corridor was washed in cold halogen light. Floor tiles clean enough to reflect faces, but empty enough to feel like the end of something.

The nurse on night rotation didn't look up when the door buzzed open.

She'd already been told — "Family."

No name. No fuss.

A figure stepped in. Hood up. Shoulders straight.

No hesitation.

Walked the full length of the hallway, boots barely touching the floor. One hand in a pocket. The other at their side, gloved.

They paused outside Room 213.

No cameras inside.

Deliberate.

No window in the door.

Strategic.

Just a number and the sound of a slow, rhythmic beep behind it — the machine measuring breath, measuring time.

The door opened.

Soft.

No creak. No click.

Inside: white sheets, the hum of oxygen flow, shadows bent by the monitor lights.

The figure stepped in. Shut the door behind them.

Didn't speak.

Just approached the bed.

One body lay still. Bandaged head. IV in both arms. Mouth slightly open. Face swollen, stitched, somewhere between recovery and the edge of nothing.

The visitor stood over the bed for a long moment.

Then…

Lowered the hood.

Still — we do not see the face.

They reached out.

Placed their hand on the patient's.

Only one word escaped their lips, and it came like smoke from a dying fire.

But we don't hear it.

They leaned down. Whispered something.

Something only the comatose man — or boy, or ghost — could ever carry.

Then they turned.

Pulled the hood back up.

And walked out the door.

The machines kept beeping.

The hand they touched did not move.

The monitor did not change.

And behind the door, the silence grew louder.

Chapter 17 - Ash And Inheritance

No funeral.

No body shown.

No name spoken.

And in London, that meant opportunity.

The Brutalists had always ruled through fear, not affection. So when silence hung over the name of the dead, the ones further from the fire began carving up territory like it was steak on a silver tray.

By Wednesday, the South Norwood crew stopped answering calls.

By Friday, the Waltham boys emptied their safehouse and didn't return.

They left the place spotless.

Like they'd never belonged to the house at all.

Someone tagged an old Brutalist wall with red paint:

"GHOSTS DON'T OWN POSTCODES."

It was cleaned within the hour.

Still, the message rang.

In Leeds, a man named Elijah Moores — cousin to someone, claim to something — sent a voice note to a known contact, saying he was "interested in adopting the out-of-town routes." He used the word "adopting" like he was doing them a favour.

Maya intercepted it.

Didn't reply.

Sariah read the transcript, flicked ash off the page, and muttered:

"Tell him if he wants custody, he can fight for it."

Meanwhile, younger crews in East London started moving unsanctioned.

Small things — untagged bags, unreported pickups, side jobs with faces from Croydon who'd once been blacklisted.

Maya took names.

Sariah didn't correct them.

Not yet.

Because chaos is truth serum.

When the power structure wobbles, everyone shows their real weight.

And the vultures don't wait for a headstone.

They start eating at the smell.

It took Maya three hours to crack the burner.

Not because of security — the phone itself was old.

Obsolete OS, no encryption.

But because whoever used it knew exactly how to cover a trail.

No contact names.

No message threads.

No stored photos.

The call log was scrubbed.

The SIM had been hot-swapped once, maybe twice.

Only one piece of data remained — a number, buried in the SIM registry. It hadn't been cleared. Maybe it was a mistake. Maybe it was intentional.

Maya ran it through her personal bank of contacts, cross-referencing old crew records from the East run.

The name pinged in her private file.

Devon Reese.

Low-level runner. Trusted. Kept his head down.

Last logged movement: July.

Status: presumed dead.

He'd gone missing after a pickup job in Poplar.

His burner went cold.

His stash car was found with blood on the seats and no gear inside.

No body.

No noise.

The assumption had been clean — he got got.

But now, his number was live.

Maya dialled it once.

It rang three times.

Then dropped.

No voicemail.

No reply.

She stared at the screen, thumb hovering over the call button again.

Instead, she hit "trace."

The signal bounced once — through a relay tower in South London — then spat back a new ping.

Edmonton.

Middle of nowhere. Derelict office parks, old printworks turned squat zones.

The call had come from inside London.

"Devon," she whispered.

Or someone using Devon's number.

She didn't call again.

She saved the number.

Slipped the burner into her drawer.

Locked it.

When she stepped out of the back room, Sariah was at the kitchen counter, sipping from a glass of something too clear to be water.

"You find anything?"

Maya hesitated.

Then nodded.

"Yeah. But not what I was hoping."

Sariah didn't press.

She just looked at her once.

Too long.

Too knowing.

And said nothing.

The old Sariah had a sense of theatre.

She wore power like silk — smooth, flexible, sharp when it needed to be.

Smiled during threats.

Paused before finishing a sentence, just to make people sweat.

That Sariah was gone.

Now she walked into the meeting room like it bored her to exist.

Three lieutenants sat around the scratched oak table in the safe flat above the old Polish deli.

Katch from Hackney.

Jonas from the East Step line.

A new one — Errol — too cocky, too casual. Sat with one leg over his knee, chewing gum like it gave him something to do with his cowardice.

Sariah didn't sit.

She stood at the head of the table, gloved hands resting on the back of the chair she never took. Her eyes scanned the room once. No folder. No phone.

Just her.

"Here's what's happening."

Her voice wasn't raised, but it cut the space like a scalpel.

"Half the house thinks the body was Kris. The other half thinks it was Ade. You three don't get to think. You follow."

Errol opened his mouth.

She didn't look at him.

"Shut it."

He did.

"Camden crew moved product without clearing it. Tell them to come home by midnight or burn with the next fire."

No reaction.

"Sol and Faheem are ghosts. Don't talk about them. Don't text them. Don't say their names near a mic."

She turned her head just slightly, eyes resting on Jonas.

"You sent two runners into Croydon last week. They weren't authorised. One of them's dead. The other's on Instagram."

Jonas blinked.

"I'll handle it."

"You won't. Spence already has. You'll apologise for wasting my time."

No one spoke.

Sariah stepped away from the chair.

"You're not here because you're smart. You're here because you haven't failed yet."

She reached the door.

Paused.

Turned back.

"You're not lieutenants. You're sandbags. If I feel water coming in, you'll be the first to drown."

Then she left.

No nod.

No goodbye.

No signal of being finished.

Just silence behind her, and three men who'd suddenly forgotten why they ever thought this job was survivable.

Rain tapped softly against the kitchen window. It wasn't enough to be dramatic — just enough to sound like someone knocking who didn't want to be let in.

Sariah sat at the small table, sleeves rolled to the elbow, scar on her right forearm white in the overhead light. She didn't look up as Maya entered.

"You check the burner?"

"Yeah."

Maya leaned against the frame, arms crossed.

"Number came back hot. Devon's."

That made Sariah pause. She still didn't look at Maya — just stared at the grain in the table like it had something to confess.

"He's dead."

"Supposed to be."

"Signal was from where?"

"Edmonton. Could've been a reroute. Could've been him. Could've been someone using him."

"And the warning call?"

"Same number that hit your burner. Logged from inside our relay. Someone internal."

Sariah nodded once.

Then finally met Maya's eyes.

"So someone warned us."

"Yeah."

"And someone planted the bomb."

"Probably not the same person."

The silence stretched.

It wasn't awkward — it was surgical. Both of them dissecting the moment, deciding what to cut open and what to let rot.

Sariah reached for her cigarette case. Silver, dented, initials scratched off.

Lit one.

Exhaled slow.

"If it came down to it," she said, "and it was one of ours behind this…"

She looked at Maya like she already knew the answer.

"Would you kill someone wearing our name?"

Maya didn't speak.

Not because she didn't know what to say —

But because she was running down the names.

Devon.

Errol.

Jonas.

Spence.

Maybe even…

"I'd think about it," she finally said.

Sariah gave a half-smile.

The kind that doesn't reach the eyes.

"Good."

She stubbed the cigarette out on the tabletop. Didn't flinch at the burn it left behind.

"Because someone already has."

Room 213 smelled like bleach and plastic.

The nurse on rotation, a soft-footed woman named Elise, entered just after four a.m. Her steps were practiced. Her hands clean. Her clipboard routine.

She didn't speak.

The monitors were steady.

O2 levels consistent.

Heart rate a flat, slow line —

Not alarming. Not improving.

She adjusted the IV.

Noticed a mild drop in the saline line pressure.

Nothing serious. Could've been a minor clot, could've been nothing.

She checked the bandages — still intact.

Then, just before she turned to go, her eyes caught it.

A movement.

Subtle.

Almost imagined.

The index finger of the patient's right hand —

not fully. Not enough to call it motion.

But it twitched.

Once.

Like a glitch in the system.

She blinked.

Waited.

The machines didn't change.

But the finger did it again.

Fraction of a second.

Then still.

Elise stepped closer.

Watched.

Held her breath.

No more movement.

She hesitated with her pen above the chart.

Then wrote nothing.

And left the room.

Behind her, the monitor beeped once.

A half-second faster than before.

Just enough to say:

Still here.

Chapter 18 - A Name Returns

He wasn't supposed to be anywhere.

Dead men don't get spotted.

Especially not in the daylight.

But that didn't stop the story.

It started with one of the younger boys — Zeek, maybe seventeen, still earning respect, still pretending he didn't flinch around gunshots. He was doing a drop near Tooting when he cut through the back of St. George's on foot, ducking CCTV, avoiding the usual traffic.

He passed by the second-floor window.

Paused.

Looked up.

What he saw made him stop breathing for a second.

Inside the hospital room — white light, blue curtain pulled — he thought he saw Kris.

Not all of him. Just a jawline. A shadow on the cheek. Bandages, yeah, but the posture…

It was the way he sat.

Or didn't sit — the way he slouched.

The way his arm dangled from the chair, fingers half-curled.

Like he didn't care if he lived or died.

Like he already knew the answer.

Zeek didn't take a photo.

Didn't think to.

He just ran.

By the time Maya heard it, the story had warped — "he stood up," "he looked at me," "he gave me a nod."

None of it could be verified.

But it didn't matter.

The word was out.

Back at the flat, one of the Stepney boys called off a run, muttering something about "waiting to see how it lands."

Another crew who hadn't checked in since the bombing suddenly started responding to texts — but only with questions.

"You lot heard?"

"He's alive, right?"

"What's the move if it's Kris?"

Maya buried her face in her hands around midnight, rubbing at the pressure in her temples.

The problem with ghosts wasn't that they haunted.

It was that they inspired loyalty.

And if Kris was alive…

He wasn't going to rebuild.

He was going to punish.

Elise didn't spook easy.

Twelve years in trauma.

Two stabbings in the staff car park.

One junkie pulled a blade on her outside A&E — she handed him a bandage and told him to hold pressure until the police came.

But that night, in Room 213, something twisted in her gut.

The room was quiet at first. Machine beep steady. No anomalies. Oxygen flow balanced.

She was just checking vitals — jotting down notes, glancing at fluid levels.

Then it came, low and wet — like a cough wrapped around a word.

She froze.

The patient twitched under the sheet, not violently, just once — shoulders shifting.

Then again, lips half-parting. Voice cracked. A rasp like stone dragging across stone.

One word first:

"Spence…"

Then nothing.

She leaned closer. Almost didn't breathe.

Then the voice came again, clearer this time, barely above a whisper, like something pulled out of a deeper layer of sleep.

"I'll rip his fuckin' jaw off…"

Her pen slipped.

She took a step back, pulse suddenly in her throat.

The voice stilled.

No movement.

The vitals didn't spike. No waking moment. Just that brief, violent echo floating in the fluorescent light.

She logged it, but didn't tell the nurse-in-charge.

Instead, she told the night orderly in a whisper outside the vending machine.

"I think he spoke."

"What'd he say?"

"Didn't catch the first bit. But the second part… it was angry."

"What kind of angry?"

She looked down at her shaking hands.

"Like he woke up mid-murder."

The orderly laughed it off. But by dawn, the story had made its way to a friend in reception, who told someone on break, who texted it to a cousin who'd once worked a job for the Brutalists.

By the time it reached Maya's phone, it was secondhand, distorted — but the core was intact.

She read the message slowly. Then again.

Then once more for the weight.

"…rip his jaw off…"

She closed the text.

Didn't tell Sariah.

She didn't need to.

Only Kris would say something like that before he'd even learned to stand again.

Spence didn't tell anyone where he was going.

He just took one of the nondescript estate cars — the black Volvo with the cracked dash — and drove east, solo. No music. No smoke. Just the ticking of the blinker when he finally turned onto the street where the fire took place.

The site was quiet now. No tape.

The council had cleared the wreckage within forty-eight hours — bent metal, melted rubber, scorched asphalt.

Even the walls had been pressure-washed.

But trauma leaves residue.

And Spence was good at spotting what most people missed.

He walked the alley twice. Once with his eyes up, once down.

The curb was still chipped.

A scorch pattern radiated from where the car had landed.

Then he saw it.

At the base of a drainpipe, tucked into the groove where pavement met brick — a glint.

It wasn't much. Could've been a coin. A bottle cap.

He crouched. Picked it up.

Not a coin.

A ring.

Charred. Warped slightly.

Still warm to the touch — or maybe that was in his head.

The face of it was dented.

But the inside was clear.

An engraving.

Small block letters. Tight spacing.

Too clean to be random.

R.M. — 14.07.03

He turned it over twice.

Kris never wore rings. Not since they were kids.

Ade? Never. Hated jewellery. Said it felt like shackles.

So whose was this?

Spence pocketed it. Didn't linger.

Drove straight back.

When he walked into the flat, Sariah was on the couch, watching a muted newsfeed scroll headlines that didn't matter.

He dropped the ring on the table in front of her.

She looked at it. Said nothing.

Spence sat down slow.

"We didn't count right."

She picked it up.

Turned it in her fingers.

Narrowed her eyes.

Not at the ring.

At the implication.

Edmonton wasn't a place you stumbled into.

You drove there for a reason.

No one wandered through the industrial stretch by chance.

Maya parked a street over, walked the last hundred yards. Hoodie up. Bag slung cross-body. Flat boots. Neutral expression. No tension in her gait — nothing to mark her as different.

The building was a converted printworks. Half-boarded. The kind of space that once pressed tabloids and now housed ghosts.

She knew the look.

Brick blistered from age. Paint tags faded under layers of rain and piss. A busted shutter gaped open, like a mouth with missing teeth.

She stepped in.

Dust.

Rotten paper.

Something dead — maybe a pigeon, maybe not.

But the back room had been lived in.

A mattress on pallets.

Food wrappers.

A scorched spoon.

Cigarette butts — same brand Devon used to smoke. Foreign, black-rolled, hard to find.

But it was the maps that made her stop.

Pinned to the wall with tape and nails.

Red thread marking routes — supply lines, maybe.

Some crossed out.

Some circled twice.

She found a small whiteboard in the corner. Erased, recently.

And next to it: a burner phone, charging off a car battery rigged through a converter.

It was still warm.

She didn't touch it.

Just took out her phone, snapped photos, logged the IMEI, pinged it to her back-channel database.

Then she saw the door at the back — a smaller one, half-hinged, warped at the base from water damage.

She opened it.

Inside, barely lit, a wall of photos.

Faces.

Some of the crew. Some not.

Some tagged with numbers.

Some with Xs.

But in the centre — right in the middle —

A printout. Grainy. CCTV still.

Kris and Ade, shoulder to shoulder, walking toward the camera. Black and white.

A single word above it:

"UNFINISHED"

Both faces had been crossed out in red marker.

Hard. Scratched deep enough to tear the paper.

Maya stared for a long time.

Then stepped back.

Left everything untouched.

Just like she found it.

Because this wasn't Devon's place.

Not anymore.

And whoever was squatting here —

They weren't looking for money.

They were building a kill list.

The room was quiet when Maya returned.

Not tired quiet — alert quiet. Like the walls were listening. Like the shadows were holding breath.

Sariah sat at the head of the table again. Spence across from her, ring still on the table between them. No drinks. No music. No movement.

Maya walked in slow. Dropped her bag. Didn't sit.

"It wasn't Devon," she said.

No one responded.

"Not in that building, anyway. But someone was living there. They knew our routes. Had maps. Strings. Our people."

She hesitated.

"There was a photo. Of the boys. Crossed out."

Still, no reaction.

Just a slow inhale from Sariah, eyes fixed ahead.

Maya opened her bag and placed a printout on the table — the CCTV still.

Faces blurred by motion.

But unmistakable.

Sariah looked at it.

Didn't touch it.

Maya leaned on the edge of the chair, voice flat.

"Whoever this is, they've been tracking us for months."

"Not us," Spence said quietly.

The first thing he'd spoken since Maya came in.

She looked at him.

"Then who?"

He tapped the image.

"Them."

Maya nodded.

"So if one's dead…"

"The other's next," Sariah finished.

A long pause.

They didn't say it.

Didn't need to.

Kris.

He was alive. They all knew it now. And he was breathing deeper every day.

Not planning.

Waiting.

Because for someone like Kris, revenge wasn't a reaction.

It was a schedule.

And when he stood up again, the only name left in his mouth…

was the one he meant to erase.

Chapter 19 - Grief With Its Teeth Still In

The first was found in Peckham.

Middle-aged. Small-time runner for a rival crew once linked to a gun charge that never stuck.

Tied to a bollard.

Face half-caved.

No witnesses.

Just a note.

Scrawled in marker across his chest, over his white shirt:

Who gave you permission to live?

No signature.

No tag.

Not even a familiar weapon.

The second showed up three days later — Walthamstow, near the old cinema.

Same method.

Same message.

Only difference was the second man had been missing for weeks.

His body was dumped at 5:27 a.m.

Traffic camera caught nothing.

Police filed both cases as "gang-related."

Didn't even knock on Brutalist doors.

They already knew what wouldn't be said.

At the house, the killings went unacknowledged.

Sariah never mentioned them.

Maya didn't write them down.

Spence made tea like the week was normal.

But something shifted.

The younger crew started saying his name again — not loud, not direct.

"Heard he's warming up."

"That wasn't a warning. That was a rhythm check."

"He's pulling strings already."

No one meant Ade.

No one ever meant Ade anymore.

Kris wasn't back.

But his mood was.

That cruel, surgical tone he took when someone needed reminding.

The way he killed not to win, but to restore narrative.

It wasn't business.

It was punctuation.

Maya read the file on the Peckham kill three times.

The note caught her eye — the way the question was phrased. Not angry. Not loud.

Just disappointed.

Spence had always kept receipts — not the kind HMRC cared about, the kind that tell you who flinched when the gun came out.

He was a watcher by nature.

Silent. Surgical.

His job wasn't to lead. It was to know who would follow, and who wouldn't.

After the second body, he started walking different routes.

He'd show up to safehouses he wasn't expected at. Sit in the back of pubs where younger crews met. Drink water. Listen. Leave before the pint hit halfway.

Back at the flat, he started testing Maya.

Small things.

Asking questions he already had answers to.

Mentioning deliveries out of sequence.

Leaving bits of false info around to see if it echoed back.

Maya didn't flinch.

But she changed, too.

Her top drawer — once half-open, a casual mess of burner logs and ciphered addresses — was now locked every time she left the room.

The laptop that used to sit on the corner of the table now travelled with her, even into the bathroom.

And when she passed Spence in the hall, she didn't nod.

Didn't speak.

Just brushed by — like they were strangers who'd once shared a war.

Something between them was fraying.

Quietly.

Almost politely.

But fraying.

Because if Kris really was alive — and if he really was behind the bodies — then someone was already helping him.

And both Maya and Spence knew that if either of them were on the wrong side of the truth…

…they wouldn't be breathing by Chapter 20.

Wednesday.

Flat above the betting shop on Barking Road.

The room was too small for the egos inside it.

Four lieutenants, three burners ringing on silent, and a bag of notes weighing down the table like a corpse that hadn't started stinking yet.

They were already halfway through the count when the lock turned.

Sariah stepped in.

No knock.

No warning.

No expression.

She wore her coat — long, black, tailored — and didn't take it off straight away.

It wasn't until she crossed the room, dropped her burner beside the stack, and hung the coat across the back of the chair that anyone noticed it.

The blood.

Lower hem. Spattered.

Not fresh, but not dry either.

Blackened at the edges.

Stiff where it had soaked through.

She didn't look at it.

Didn't explain.

She just sat.

Rolled up her sleeves.

Pulled a pen from her jacket.

"You're two short on the East drop," she said flatly.

Katch tried to speak.

"We moved—"

"I know what you moved. I'm telling you what you missed."

Silence.

She started flicking through the stack of receipts.

Made no comment about the rest.

No one brought up the coat.

Not the lieutenants.

Not the runner waiting by the door with a USB full of burner logs.

Not even Jonas, who usually couldn't shut up if someone was actually on fire.

They all saw it.

They all swallowed it.

Because in that moment, it didn't matter if Kris was coming back.

What mattered was Sariah was already here.

And no one in the room wanted to find out if the blood was hers…

or someone else's.

The call came through a ghost line — one of the old numbers Maya kept live for tracing ex-affiliates who didn't know they were still on the radar.

7:13 p.m.

Coded out of a pub bathroom in Woolwich.

Two voices. Young. Anxious but not stupid.

She patched into the audio.

Didn't interrupt.

"She's still sitting at the top, yeah?"

"Sariah?"

"Yeah."

"For now."

"You think that's solid?"

"Nah. She's a placeholder. We all know who's really gonna run it."

"If he comes back."

"He's not coming back. He's already here. Just not dressed yet."

Maya's finger hovered over the record button.

She didn't press it.

"I heard he's got a list."

"Course he does."

"She's on it?"

"She built the list. He's just gonna finish it."

Laughter.

Not joyful — just brittle.

The call dropped after forty seconds.

Disconnected at the source.

Maya sat back. Closed the file.

Didn't trace it.

Didn't log it.

Didn't tell Spence.

She simply deleted the audio from the buffer.

Not because she believed them.

But because part of her did.

And that part was getting louder every time someone whispered his name.

The click of the drawer was soft, but Maya's ears had been tuned to suspicion for weeks.

She froze halfway down the hall, one hand still damp from washing blood — not hers — off her forearms. Paused. Tilted her head.

Another click.

Not the lock.

The USB port cover.

She moved quiet. Barefoot. Breath shallow.

The living room was lit only by the lamp in the corner.

Spence sat at her desk. Back hunched. Elbows tight.

He thought she was out.

He thought wrong.

She didn't interrupt.

Just leaned against the wall, shadowed, watching.

His hand moved the mouse across her private drive — a folder labeled "MAYA-D2-REDACTED."

Encrypted. Obscured. Still there.

He couldn't open it. Not without her password.

But he was trying.

And trying meant one thing: he didn't trust her.

After a moment, he closed the lid.

Didn't notice her.

Didn't turn.

He stood.

Picked up his burner from the table — except, he didn't.

Left it behind by mistake. Or maybe on purpose.

Maya waited until the door clicked shut behind him.

Then crossed the room.

The burner was unlocked.

Not something Spence ever did.

A single draft message sat on the screen.

Unsent. Half-typed.

I don't think it was a bomb meant for both of them.

No recipient listed.

No timestamp.

Just those words.

Staring back like a confession.

Maya read it twice.

Then three times.

She didn't delete it.

She didn't tell Sariah.

She just sat there in the dim glow, the cursor blinking after that sentence —

like it was waiting for someone to reply.

Chapter 20 - The One With His Eyes Open

He opened his eyes like he'd only blinked.

No panic.

No alarms.

No beeping escalation.

Just silence. A pause. Then a single exhale from somewhere deep inside his chest — not pain, not relief, just breath. The first recorded since the explosion, according to the chart clipped to the bed.

The nurse on rotation didn't notice it immediately. Her back was to him, charting fluids, running through motions she'd repeated a hundred nights before on people who never came back.

Until he said:

"Oi."

She flinched.

Spun.

Stared.

Kris was awake.

Eyes open, focused. Lips split and dry but already curling into the shape of a demand.

"Where's my coat?"

That was it.

No "where am I."

No "what happened."

No "is he alive?"

Just the coat.

The nurse stepped back toward the bed. Slowly. Like she was afraid to break the moment.

"Sir— I need to— you've been in a—"

He raised a hand.

Wires tugged. IV hissed.

Then he gripped the line and ripped it out.

Clean. Fast. No flinch.

"I asked," he said, voice cracked but calm, "where's my fuckin' coat."

She didn't answer.

He sat up.

Didn't wobble.

Didn't groan.

Just planted his feet on the cold floor and flexed his hands like a man remembering the shape of violence.

His palms were bandaged. His side bruised.

But he stood.

Weight on both legs. Spine upright. Face blank.

He walked three steps to the sink.

Looked in the mirror.

Didn't react to what he saw — stitched temple, blood-crusted hair, a face thinned out by days unconscious.

He ran a hand down his jaw. Felt the old scar.

Then gripped the metal railing of the sink.

He stayed like that for a while.

When the nurse returned, he was dressed — hospital trousers, plain shirt. Shoes he'd found by the bed. The hospital gown was folded neatly on the chair.

She tried again.

"Sir, please… you've been unconscious for days. We need to—"

"I'm done sleeping."

That was all he said before walking back to the window.

Back straight. Shoulders high.

Like a man not recovering…

…but returning.

Her name was Nadira, twenty-nine, twelve-hour shifts, four cups of tea between midnight and morning. She'd seen burns, bullet wounds, the slow wasting of men who thought death was a debt that came for others.

But this one…

This one didn't come back like the rest.

He didn't gasp, didn't cry out, didn't grab at his chest or try to name someone lost.

He sat.

Then he stood.

Then he looked out the window like he knew exactly what street he was on — and more importantly, who else was on it.

When she handed him water, his fingers brushed hers.

Cold.

Calloused.

Too calm for someone who'd just survived being blown apart.

She tried small talk.

"You've been through a lot."

No reply.

"You were unconscious. Fire injuries. Head trauma…"

He blinked.

"You had no ID on you. Ambulance said you were found near—"

He turned his head then. Slowly. Not all the way. Just enough for his eyes to find hers.

That stare—

It froze her.

Not because it was angry.

Because it was familiar.

Like he knew her. Not from this life, maybe not even from this city, but in that moment she felt like her name was written behind his eyes.

She stepped back.

He looked away.

Didn't speak again.

She finished her notes with shaky hands. Left the room without even giving him his meds.

Later, in the security lounge, she told the guard on shift:

"He's awake. Calm. Like… like a statue that knew when to come alive."

"You okay?"

She paused.

"I think he recognised me."

"You've seen him before?"

She shook her head.

"No."

"So what makes you say that?"

She didn't answer right away.

Then finally, softly:

"Because when he looked at me, I felt like I owed him something."

The guard didn't write it down.

Didn't need to.

By the end of the night, three orderlies, two nurses, and one cleaner knew a man on Floor 2 had survived a bomb with no ID, no visitors, and a stare that made your lungs forget how to work.

They didn't know his name.

But the hallways ran colder after he woke up.

Spence was the kind of quiet that made people forget he was even in the room.

That's why when he wasn't where he was supposed to be — you noticed.

It was Maya who clocked it first.

They were supposed to meet at 3 p.m. to clear ledger discrepancies.

He didn't show.

Didn't answer calls.

Didn't ping his location.

Didn't offer an excuse when she finally saw him again around half six, coming in through the back door of the safehouse like nothing had happened.

Only… something had.

His hoodie was soaked through at the collar and sleeve, clinging to his chest. Not rain. Not sweat.

Something thicker.

His right hand — bare knuckles, split.

No wrapping.

No cleaning.

Fresh skin torn where he'd clearly driven it into bone.

He walked straight to the sink, ran the cold tap, shoved his hands under.

Didn't speak.

Maya didn't ask.

She stood by the door, arms folded, watching him scrub like he was trying to peel history off the creases of his palms.

When he was done, he grabbed a towel.

Wrapped it around both hands.

Tossed it toward the laundry basket, missed.

She didn't move.

"You were gone three hours."

No answer.

"Didn't check in."

Still nothing.

He peeled off the hoodie next, revealing a faint streak across his ribs — a smear, maybe blood, maybe not. He turned away before she could read more.

"We done?" he muttered, without looking at her.

"For now."

He left the room without turning back.

Later, when he was upstairs, Maya opened the bin beneath the sink.

The towel was there.

Folded. Quiet.

Its inner layer streaked red, like a fingerprint confession.

She stared at it.

Didn't pull it out.

Didn't report it.

Because if Spence was washing blood off his hands…

she needed to know whose.

And whether the blood had screamed when it hit the floor.

No one discharged him.

There was no form signed.

No clipboard.

No nurse wheeling him down with a lukewarm smile and a plastic bag of belongings.

Kris got up at 2:11 a.m.

Put on the plain white tee they'd left folded on the chair.

Hospital trousers swapped for a pair of black jeans — slightly too long in the leg — taken from a laundry bin in the ward hallway.

The boots were laced with surgical tubing.

Tight. Precise.

The coat?

Dark.

Wool.

Expensive.

Not his.

Someone else's.

Maybe a visitor's. Maybe a body's.

He pulled it on slow, pausing only to check the fit in the window's reflection.

It draped over him perfectly, the collar up, the sleeves folded just once at the cuff — like he'd worn it before in another life.

His face was paler now.

Sunken at the cheekbones.

But the eyes...

The eyes were worse.

Not wild.

Not angry.

Cold.

When he stepped through the fire exit — smooth, unhurried, the alarm already disabled with a borrowed keycard — he didn't look back.

He didn't take his chart.

Didn't take meds.

Didn't take anything but the skin he'd grown back into and the silence that now trailed behind him like a second shadow.

At 2:48 a.m., a CCTV camera outside a shuttered chemist caught him crossing the street.

No limp.

No stagger.

No hesitation.

Just walk.

Measured. Heavy. Like every footstep knew where it was going — and who would be waiting at the end of the route.

And on that grainy, flickering feed, just before he turned the corner and vanished into the east London dark…

Kris lifted his head…

…and smiled.

Chapter 21 - All Of This Is Still Mine

The fire started just before dawn.

Three blocks east of Bow Road, in a terrace squat the crews used for dry holds — clean, low-risk, quiet.

The locals said they smelled petrol around 4 a.m.

By 4:07, flames were licking through the boarded windows like teeth behind rotting lips.

When the fire brigade arrived, they found one man still breathing inside.

Dev Malik.

Ex-runner. Turned talker.

Sariah had kept him around longer than she should've — said he was a "known quantity."

Kris always said: "known" just means you know where the blade's coming from.

They dragged Dev out wrapped in foil, skin blackened, eyes pink with smoke. He wasn't talking. Couldn't. His throat was cooked dry.

But someone had left him a message.

Stapled through his jacket pocket — right through the fabric, high and brutal — was a photograph.

Crisp. Unburned. Fresh print.

Sariah and Dev.

Sitting at a table.

From maybe six months ago. Maybe less.

Sariah mid-smile.

Dev looking down at something — a notepad?

Or cash?

The picture wasn't captioned. Wasn't signed.

But there was a line drawn across the table with a thick black marker. Diagonal. From her hand to his.

A cut.

An accusation.

Or a boundary.

The fire didn't kill Dev.

But it did the job.

By the time word reached the house, three other defectors had already gone underground.

One left a message in a pub toilet stall in Whitechapel:

"He's alive. And he's not talking. He's telling."

Because this was Kris's language.

Not speeches.

Not threats.

Just smoke, scars, and silence that spelled your name in ash.

The message came without a signature —

just a single word, dropped in each burner:

"Now."

No location.

But they all knew where.

The flat above Harwood's, her inherited fortress. Once Ade's.

Now unmistakably hers.

Five arrived. No more.

No plus-ones. No whisperers from the lower ranks. This wasn't a council.

It was a show of possession.

Spence took the seat nearest the window.

Maya sat across from him, unreadable.

Katch — mouth always half open like he wanted to speak but knew better — perched at the edge of his chair.

Reya came last.

The fifth was new — mid-thirties, pale, tattoos half-scrubbed, name unknown. Sariah's pet project, apparently.

Sariah stood for a long moment before sitting.

Her coat was off. Black blouse. Rings off. Nails clean.

Only thing she wore was the look.

The one that said I will bury the next person who interrupts me.

She didn't ask how they were. Didn't welcome them.

Just sat. Lifted a tumbler of dark liquor. Didn't sip.

"Someone's burning old furniture," she said, calm. "Trying to smoke out ghosts."

Silence.

"Let him."

Spence didn't blink.

Maya didn't shift.

Katch dropped his gaze.

"I don't care who's alive. If he wants the table back—"

She placed the glass down, hard enough to clink.

"Tell him to crawl."

No one moved.

But everyone looked at her hand.

Knuckles white around the glass.

Tendons tight.

Like she was holding something down.

Not rage.

Not grief.

Fear.

She might not say it.

But she felt it.

Because even the boldest voice in a house knows when the walls remember a different king.

Spence didn't speak the whole meeting.

Didn't twitch. Didn't blink out of rhythm. Just sat, legs crossed, one hand loose around the base of his glass, the other resting on his knee like a man waiting for weather to change.

When it ended, he was the last to leave.

He took his time with the stairs — slow, deliberate. Lit a cigarette outside with a match, not a lighter. That old habit he only used when he was thinking too hard to trust muscle memory.

He didn't walk home.

He walked east. Two blocks. Cut through a snicket that used to house side deals. Entered the back of a shuttered bar that hadn't served a drink in years.

Inside: dust, mold, silence.

He pulled a burner from his coat pocket.

Not the one everyone knew about.

The real one.

Pressed a number. No ID. No label.

One ring.

Two.

Then:

"Yeah."

Spence exhaled slowly.

"She's cracking."

A beat.

"Don't push."

Another pause.

"Let her swing first."

Then he ended the call.

Didn't wait for a reply.

Didn't even pocket the phone — just dropped it behind the bar and crushed it under his boot.

One sharp twist.

Plastic snapped. Battery hissed.

Spence didn't flinch.

He walked out the way he came.

Didn't light another smoke.

And when he passed the old mural on the corner — faded image of a lion with a crown — he looked up at it.

Not with respect.

With recognition.

Because Spence wasn't picking a side in the war…

He'd already picked.

And he was just waiting for the noise to start.

She waited until dusk.

Not night — too easy to clock. Not morning — too many witnesses. Dusk. The hour when things blur, when the shadows stretch and nothing looks guilty enough to stop.

The storage yard was quiet.

Same rusted keypad. Same security camera hanging limp.

Same flicker of a motion light that didn't come on unless you made it angry.

Maya keyed into Unit 49.

No extra steps. No hesitation.

She rolled up the shutter and stared.

Empty.

The crates were gone.

No guns.

No cash.

No burner.

Only dust prints on the floor where the heavy crates had sat. Wide. Military-style. Recently moved — maybe the night before, maybe this morning.

She stepped inside. Checked the walls.

One new thing: a nail in the brickwork, bent slightly downward.

Nothing hanging from it.

But it was fresh. Too clean to have been here when she came last.

She didn't say a word.

Just shut the door, locked it, and walked two blocks to an internet café with no cameras and a broken toilet.

She checked Reya's last known burner ping.

Dead.

Not powered off. Wiped.

No movement. No new pings.

Off the grid.

And Reya never moved without being told. Which meant someone higher was giving her orders.

Maya didn't call Sariah.

She didn't call anyone.

She just sat at a plastic desk in a place that smelled like fried cables and old sugar, and stared at the blank screen of her laptop.

People were arming up.

But not for protection.

They weren't preparing for war with Manchester.

That was over.

They were preparing for something closer.

Internal. Personal.

The guns were back.

And they had new owners.

The café didn't open to the public.

No sign. No hours. No menus. Just a boarded-over shopfront near Leytonstone with a cracked window and one loyal camera aimed not at the door, but the pavement across the road.

Inside, only one man.

Call him Darren Cole.

Used to run with the old dockyard lot. Slipped out clean. No heat, no prison time — just one of those men who knew when to become invisible.

At 3:17 a.m., the back door clicked open.

Darren didn't look up from the espresso he never finished.

He didn't need to.

"Kris," he said, without turning.

The chair across from him scraped once.

No answer.

Kris sat.

Still wearing that coat. No bruises showing. No smile.

He didn't put his hands on the table. Didn't touch the cup Darren slid toward him. Just sat there, breathing like someone who'd figured out exactly how many people he was going to have to kill and when.

Darren cleared his throat.

"You look good."

Nothing.

"I heard… well. Lot of people heard. That you—"

Still silence.

"You here to talk or tally?"

That got a reaction — just one.

Kris leaned forward, just an inch.

Boot dragged slowly through the dust on the tiled floor. Drew a long, deliberate line between them.

Then he stood.

Left without a word.

Didn't look back.

Darren stared at the line in the dirt like it was ink on a death certificate.

By dawn, he'd cleared the shop. Burned the contact logs. Told his crew to disappear. No excuses, no delay.

Because Kris hadn't left a message.

He'd left a boundary.

And Darren knew — like everyone else now knew:

Kris was drawing his world back, one line at a time.

Chapter 22 - Soft Targets And Family Names

He hadn't worn colours in years.

Didn't run pickups. Didn't clear drops. Didn't show face at any table that still bore the name. He lived quiet — flat in Clapton, food delivery gigs, Sunday phone calls to his mum.

His name was Darius Webb.

Used to be called Brick back in Ade's days. Reliable. Built like a freezer. Retired after the second raid on the Romford crew when Sariah started taking command.

No enemies. No debts. Just memories.

That's why when the jogger found him half-buried in leaves off the trail in Hackney Marshes, the shock wasn't that he was hurt…

It was how specific the violence was.

His arms were broken — both.

Nose flattened.

Jaw split.

Teeth missing.

But his throat was untouched.

And on his left forearm, someone had carved a word:

BRUTAL

Not written. Not tattooed.

Carved.

Deep.

Ugly.

Just above the faded tattoo of the family crest: a broken crown over a steel rose. The ink was thirty years old — almost gone.

But the new word was fresh.

Red. Raised. Deliberate.

Whoever did it hadn't meant to kill him.

They meant to send him.

He was found alive — barely.

No wallet.

Phone smashed.

But in his mouth, stuffed deep into the gap where teeth used to be, was a scrap of black cloth.

It wasn't a gang rag.

It was part of an old coat lining — the type only one person used to wear.

One brother.

And everyone who saw it, even the cops who didn't know what they were looking at, said the same thing:

"This wasn't random."

Because when Kris made a move…

he didn't waste the bullet.

He used your skin.

The room was tight and low-ceilinged, carpet still soaked with spilled rum from a fight that'd happened weeks earlier. No one cleaned it. The stink kept lower ranks from hanging around too long.

Sariah liked it for meetings.

No chairs. No table. Just her, Maya, and Spence standing close enough to smell the sweat off each other's nerves.

She started with no greeting.

Just:

"One of ours got dug out the dirt."

Maya said nothing.

Spence folded his arms.

"Old name," Sariah added. "Didn't matter anymore."

"Clearly it did to someone," Maya said.

Sariah nodded once.

"Yeah. The someone who's walking around like he's got permission."

She took a step closer. A little too close.

"He doesn't."

Spence shifted. Not much. But enough.

"So we hit back?"

Sariah's mouth twitched. Could've been a smile. Could've been something sharper.

"No. We watch."

She tossed a burner onto a cracked sideboard. Screen already lit. A name: Elijah Marris.

Ex-runner. Middle tier. Still got teeth. Still loyal, supposedly.

"He's been meeting people that don't drink where we drink."

"You want him tailed?" Maya asked.

"I want to know if he's spreading my name around like it's a discount code."

Spence spoke up, low:

"He's not a threat."

"Neither was Darius," she snapped.

"We don't tail everyone who used to take orders."

"We do now."

Spence stared at her.

She met it, unflinching.

"You all want control," she said. "I want order. You know the difference?"

No one answered.

She turned to leave.

Before she did, she said:

"Send Maya. Keep her close. I want eyes, not blood."

Then paused at the door.

"For now."

The room stayed quiet long after she'd gone.

The smell of that sticky carpet rising like something spoiled.

Spence stayed behind.

Didn't look at Maya when he finally muttered:

"She's hunting shadows."

"Or calling them," Maya replied.

The car park in Whitechapel had been condemned since 2021.

Still stood. Concrete rot holding firm.

No cameras. No patrols. Just a view of the city like a dying god's balcony — wide, empty, full of ghosts.

Spence waited alone on the top level. Hood up. Hands in pockets. The wind whipped sharp off the Thames.

The contact was late by three minutes. That mattered.

Spence clocked it.

When they arrived, it wasn't with a handshake or a name.

Just a nod.

A body language both of them knew too well —

We've done things. We're doing one more.

Spence pulled out a small burner wrapped in a sandwich bag.

Clean. Fresh. Untraceable.

He handed it over.

"Same number as last time," he said. "Same rule — burn it after you hear his voice."

The contact didn't speak. Just nodded again.

Then Spence pulled out a second slip of paper. Folded once, no name on the outside.

He held it up. Let the wind threaten to take it.

Then passed it over.

The contact opened it.

Read the name.

Raised an eyebrow — slightly.

It wasn't Sariah's.

It was a man most had forgotten.

Alfie Ridge.

Ex-fixer.

Disappeared after the Clapham Disassembly — one of the last people to ever walk away from Kris and Ade with all their fingers intact.

The contact looked up.

"He still breathin'?"

Spence gave a half-smile.

"Barely."

"Why him?"

Spence flicked his cigarette away.

"Because he knows what we were like… before her."

He turned to leave.

"And because if she's gonna start watching people — I want someone watching back."

He didn't say Sariah's name.

Didn't have to.

Some names hiss even when whispered.

St. Joseph's Trauma Ward didn't ask too many questions.

Not at 4:12 a.m.

Not when the visitor had the right name, the right date of birth, the right signature on the intake form.

And not when they said they were "cousin on the father's side — twice removed, but raised close."

The nurse waved him through.

Darius Webb lay unconscious.

One arm in a brace, his jaw wired shut, half his face stitched like it had been unzipped and reluctantly sewn back.

He hadn't spoken since arriving.

Wouldn't for weeks — maybe longer.

But someone thought he might.

The visitor was tall. Pale hoodie. Leather gloves despite the heat.

Didn't speak.

Didn't sit.

Just stood at the foot of the bed.

Watched the slow rise of Darius's chest.

Watched the way the eyes beneath bruised lids fluttered like they were still trying to wake up from what happened in the trees.

Then the visitor moved.

Walked to the side.

Took Darius's left hand gently, like a lover might.

Slipped something into it.

A folded note.

Pressed it into the curled fingers.

Then left, silent.

Didn't sign out.

Didn't even look at the nurse on the way out.

When they found the note two hours later during a linen change, the nurse opened it.

Seven words.

"Speak again and I'll take your teeth."

One at a time.

No signature.

No handwriting ID.

Just black marker, pressed down hard, like it had been written with more wrist than pen.

Security checked the cameras.

They were down.

Three hours of footage wiped.

No one admitted to the floor.

No one seen leaving.

Just the man in the bed…

…and the name no one dared write on the chart,

but everyone whispered in the hallway like a prayer you didn't want answered.

Kris.

Not trying to stay hidden.

Just reminding people what happened when you carried the name wrong.

The cab smelled like bacon rolls and old ash.

The kind of scent that clung to everything but couldn't be sold.

Kris sat in the back.

Right corner. Hood up. Leg crossed.

His coat was different now — grey wool, sharp cut.

Not a gangster's coat.

A mourner's.

The driver was talkative. East End accent, edges worn dull.

"You from round here?"

Kris didn't answer.

"I clocked you when you stepped out. That walk, y'know? Like someone owed you pavement."

Still nothing.

The driver tapped the meter. Flicked a glance up.

"Used to see blokes like you down by Albert Docks. Real ones. Before all that Brutalist lot started flashin' teeth like they'd built the road themselves."

A pause.

Then:

"You run with them, didn't you? Back in the day?"

Long silence.

Then Kris said — soft, almost a whisper:

"They were just borrowing the name."

The cabbie laughed like it was a joke.

Then saw Kris's eyes in the rearview.

And stopped laughing.

"Right. Yeah. I get you."

Kris looked out the window.

Watched a kid on a bike fail to cross before the lights changed.

"You do anything now?" the driver asked. "I mean— workwise?"

Another pause.

Then:

"Nothing anymore."

The driver nodded like that made perfect sense.

Didn't ask again.

They drove the rest of the way in silence.

But the mirror told a different story.

Because Kris didn't look tired. Or lost. Or sick.

He looked surgical.

Like he wasn't driving toward something.

He was driving back.

Chapter 23 - Hard Rain Doesn't Ask

Lenny Blake had been with the family since back when the word Brutalist was still said with teeth, not paperwork.

He was a listener. A connector.

Never top brass, never a soldier — just the kind of man who knew how to link people together without them noticing the strings.

But when you string the wrong people too close, eventually you're the one who gets pulled apart.

The car was a Honda. Beige. Boring.

Left parked half a block from the Bethnal Green boxing gym, engine cold, no signs of forced entry.

The window was slightly down, like he might've been waiting for someone.

They found him at 6:23 a.m.

Dead.

Still seated upright, belt buckled.

His lips were sewn shut.

Not stitched clean like a surgeon might.

Sloppy. Rough.

Like someone had yanked dental floss through the skin with a rusted upholstery needle.

His hands were folded neatly in his lap.

And in those hands—

A single sheet of paper.

Folded once.

Maya opened it at the scene.

Recognised the handwriting.

Lenny's.

Five names. All written by him.

All people he had vouched for over the years.

Some still inside. Some drifted. One dead.

At the bottom of the page, not in Lenny's hand, was one line in thick black marker:

"Your word doesn't mean anything anymore."

Maya didn't show Sariah the list.

She didn't have to.

Because when she called it in, Sariah didn't ask for who, or where, or how.

Just said:

"It was him."

"You don't know that."

"No one else would stitch a mouth just to make a point."

Maya didn't argue.

And in her silence, Sariah heard something worse than agreement.

She heard confirmation.

The room was a butcher's shop that hadn't seen meat in a decade.

Now it just stank of bleach, blood ghosts, and bad decisions.

Spence stood at the head of the table — not like a boss, more like someone asking to borrow peace.

Not one person in the room made eye contact longer than five seconds.

To his left: Delroy Triggs.

One of the last old-schoolers still loyal to Sariah — not because he liked her, but because her name paid his bills faster.

To his right: Kevan 'Two-Hour' Shaw.

Never said where he got the nickname, but he'd been seen with Kris two nights back, sitting quiet at a bar no one else in the room had the stones to walk into.

Spence cleared his throat.

"This ain't the time for split camps," he said. "There's too many enemies and not enough of us left with working lungs."

Delroy sneered.

"Funny, comin' from a bloke who only shows up when things need patchin'."

Kevan laughed softly.

Didn't speak. Just kept flipping a cigarette between his fingers like he was timing something.

Spence sighed.

"Look, none of you trust each other. Fine. Don't have to. Just stop bleeding on each other's doorsteps."

Delroy leaned forward.

"You tryin' to speak for her, Spence? Or for him?"

"I'm speakin' for what's left of us."

Silence.

Then Kevan reached into his pocket.

The room stiffened.

But all he pulled out was a folding blade.

Slim. Clean. Familiar.

He opened it slowly.

Placed it gently on the centre of the table.

"Here's my trust," he said. "Right there."

And walked out.

Didn't look back.

Didn't take the knife.

Delroy stared at it for a long moment.

Then turned to Spence.

"He walks like he knows where the next body's going."

Spence didn't reply.

Because he didn't know if Kevan was warning them…

Or if he'd just named himself the next one due.

Maya was never interested in violence.

She studied patterns.

And patterns never bled — they just repeated until someone paid attention.

That's why she noticed it:

Four linked wire transfers. All to a shell account with no name, only a number.

£18,000. Then £22,000. Then £7,000. Then £44,000 — the last one two days ago.

All drawn from side-hustle accounts Sariah didn't even know still existed.

Old Ade slush money, stashed behind expired property leases and phantom phone contracts.

Maya followed the trail to Mitcham.

Industrial estate, dead-end road, single-entry gate.

Closed off to the world — unless you had Reya's clearance code, which she did.

Inside, a crate sat in storage bay 6B.

No label. No paperwork.

She cracked it open.

Guns.

Not street-level junk.

Imported Eastern bloc stuff. Modern. Wrapped in oil cloth. Untouched.

More than that — new.

Not from the family's past.

Not even from their usual ports.

This was someone else's pipeline.

And the kicker?

The lease on the storage unit had been prepaid six months in advance…

By a company that didn't officially exist.

The company's listed contact?

Dax Turner.

A name Maya hadn't heard since her earliest days under Ade.

A broker, not a soldier.

The kind of man who sold structure, not product.

Known for one thing:

Building gangs from broken pieces — then cashing out before the blood hit the bricks.

She shut the crate.

Didn't touch the weapons again.

On her way out, she passed the mirror by the front desk.

Didn't recognise the face she saw.

Eyes sharper than she remembered.

Mouth set too flat.

Because if Reya was funneling money to Dax —

then someone else was writing a new name for the streets south of the river…

…and the Brutalists weren't invited.

The flat above Harwood's was empty except for two voices and too many ghosts.

Sariah stood by the window, arms crossed, blazer half-buttoned like she'd put it on mid-argument and never finished dressing.

Spence leaned against the kitchen counter, drinking coffee that had long gone cold.

"You knew, didn't you?" she said.

No venom in it. Just pressure. Like a blade tip against the ribs.

Spence stared into the mug.

"Knew what?"

"Lenny was talking to both sides."

He didn't blink.

"I suspected."

"And you didn't tell me?"

"I didn't know what side I was on."

Sariah turned.

Fast. Sharp.

"You arrogant bastard."

She stepped in close. The smell of tobacco and lavender soap.

"You think you're better than all of us because you don't carry a blade or pull a trigger? You think that makes you clean?"

Spence didn't flinch.

Didn't move.

"You loved Ade," he said quietly. "But Kris? You just wanted him to worship you."

That was when it came.

Crack.

Her open hand across his cheek.

Loud. Real.

Felt like the room stopped moving.

Spence blinked once.

Didn't touch his face.

Sariah's voice broke, but only once.

"You're a coward in a family of monsters."

She left.

Boot heels on wood.

Door slammed.

No echo.

Spence exhaled slow.

Finished the coffee.

Still didn't move.

Because he'd just realised something—

He might not be the monster.

But he wasn't anything else, either.

Katch never missed a check-in.

He was old-school like that.

Didn't do voice notes, didn't like texting, just showed up. Boots loud, attitude louder.

Loyal to Sariah from the start.

Because when Ade died, he needed to believe someone still deserved his fists.

But this time — nothing.

No calls.

No sightings.

No whisper of trouble.

Just… gone.

They found his boots at 10:46 p.m., outside his old flat in Holloway.

Place had been empty for years — Katch hadn't lived there since the last arson scare.

But someone had left them there, side by side.

Not kicked off.

Not dropped.

Placed.

Boots polished, laces tied neatly.

The left one even had the sole cleaned — something Katch never did.

No blood.

No scuff marks.

No note.

Just absence, dressed up like ceremony.

Maya was the first to arrive.

She stood there, staring at them in the porch light, hands in her coat.

Didn't move for nearly a minute.

Then she said quietly:

"No one else could've got that close."

The others didn't reply.

Didn't have to.

Because whether Katch left on his own…

…or someone made him leave…

the boots were a message.

And everyone who saw them knew what it meant:

Another one's gone quiet.

And if Katch — the most brutal loyalist Sariah had — didn't think she was worth standing behind anymore…

…then maybe it wasn't a war between people anymore.

Maybe it was just a collapse, slow and silent.

One boot at a time.

Chapter 24 - The Girl With The Gun In Her Mouth

Her name was Alina Ward.

Nineteen.

Studied English Lit at Queen Mary's.

Didn't carry knives. Didn't drink. Walked everywhere with her earbuds in and her backpack zipped to the top.

She wasn't part of the game.

Not even on the same street.

But her father, Jon Ward, was.

Mid-level affiliate. Moved money and product quiet for Sariah through his cleaning business. Kept his head down. Thought it made him invisible.

He was wrong.

She was taken at 4:12 p.m.

Not a snatch and grab.

Not a rush or a scream.

Just a white van on Galesmoor Road.

Two men. Calm. One watching, one moving.

She was gone in ten seconds.

The CCTV caught nothing.

But Alina remembered everything.

They put a bag over her head, sat her in a chair, didn't tie her.

Didn't say a word for twenty minutes.

Then someone came in. Alone.

She could hear his boots.

The click of a lighter.

The scrape of a metal chair dragged across the floor.

Then:

"Here."

Something cold pressed into her palm.

"You know what that is?"

She nodded. Couldn't breathe.

"Put it in your mouth."

She didn't move.

"Not loaded," he said. "Not yet."

She did as she was told.

The gun was cold. Barrel rough with scratches.

She held it between her teeth like glass.

"Good. Now sit still. If it shakes, someone dies."

She didn't know how long it lasted.

Five minutes. Ten. Maybe more.

When it was over, he took the gun back.

Didn't touch her.

Didn't say anything else.

Just left the room.

She was dropped off two hours later on a residential street in silence.

She didn't scream. Didn't run.

She just walked into the nearest police station with shaking hands and said:

"I think I was supposed to die."

The detective asked if she saw his face.

"No."

But when asked what he sounded like, she said:

"He never raised his voice. He just… sounded like someone who's already made peace with whatever he's about to do."

Later, when the recording was played for Sariah, she stood up halfway through and walked out.

Because the detective didn't know who he was describing.

But she did.

Kris.

And worse —

He didn't want revenge.

He wanted her to feel it.

Jon Ward didn't knock.

He walked straight into the safehouse office on Westmount Lane like a man already mid-sentence.

Sariah looked up from the burner she was torching.

Maya stood behind her, eyes narrow.

Spence sat in the corner, sipping tea like he'd never left.

Jon's face was wrong.

Not angry. Not broken.

Just… gone.

Pale, hollowed, shaking through the fingers but not the voice.

"I'm out," he said.

Sariah didn't move.

"Out of what?"

"All of it."

"You think there's an off-switch?"

"I don't care. I'm done."

"He threatened your daughter."

"He didn't threaten her," Jon said, voice wobbling now. "He could've done worse. Should've. That would've made sense."

He stepped forward.

Not defiant — just exhausted.

"But he didn't touch her. Didn't scream. Didn't flinch. Just made her hold it."

He looked Sariah in the eye.

"He gave her a choice in how scared she wanted to be. That's the worst kind of punishment."

Silence filled the room like water through broken stone.

Sariah stood slowly.

"You're walking away because he showed mercy?"

"No," Jon said. "I'm walking away because he doesn't care about rules anymore. Not yours. Not mine."

She took a step forward. Spence shifted in his chair.

"You're a coward," she said.

"No," Jon whispered. "I'm a father."

He left.

The door closed without a sound.

Sariah turned to Spence.

"Say it. Go on."

Spence didn't.

Not right away.

Then:

"He's not scared of Kris."

He stood now, eyes locked with hers.

"He's scared of what Kris is willing to walk away from."

Sariah's jaw flexed.

Maya didn't speak.

Just glanced at the burner phone on the table.

Still warm.

Still burning.

And somewhere on the other end of whatever line Kris wasn't using…

…another name was probably already in his mouth.

The Westmount safehouse had rules.

No shouting. No weapons drawn. No names above whispers.

That morning, Sariah broke all three.

She stormed in before sunrise, coat soaked from rain, mascara bled into her eyes, boots still muddy from wherever she'd been the night before.

Maya was by the door.

Didn't speak.

Didn't need to.

She just stepped out of the way.

Sariah went for the lockers.

Started throwing things — burner phones, files, a Glock she didn't check for a round.

"He's in the walls," she muttered. "He's in the f***ing walls."

Maya stayed still.

"You think someone's feeding him?" she asked, calm.

"I know it," Sariah snapped. "He's never this clean. Never this precise. He's getting tipped."

She turned to the first lieutenant that walked in — a wide-eyed runner named Clarke.

"Out."

"I—"

"You're out. You're done. Don't come near my crew again."

He hesitated. Then left.

The second lieutenant, Vell, tried to argue.

"I've been with you since Ade—"

"Exactly," she snarled. "And he's dead. Maybe you should've gone with him."

Vell didn't say another word.

He just turned and walked — head down, back stiff, like if he looked behind him, he'd vanish too.

Spence entered halfway through the chaos.

Didn't speak.

Didn't interrupt.

He just watched.

Sariah grabbed a burner and hurled it at the far wall. It shattered.

"I'm not stupid," she said, to no one. "I know he's not getting lucky. He knows where we sleep, what we move, who we trust."

Her voice cracked now.

"Someone's bleeding the map."

Maya finally spoke:

"Or maybe he doesn't need the map anymore."

That stopped everything.

For three seconds.

Sariah turned.

"You sayin' he's smarter than me?"

"I'm saying he's looser than you."

Silence again.

Sariah didn't reply.

Just walked into the back room, slammed the door behind her.

Spence looked at Maya.

"She's burning furniture to catch ghosts."

Maya didn't smile.

Didn't blink.

She just whispered back:

"And ghosts don't burn."

Spence lived out of an old betting shop now.

No signage. No machines. Just dust and silence.

He said he liked the quiet — but what he really liked was the isolation.

No crew. No kids running bags.

Just one wall, torn calendar still pinned to it, dates scribbled in blue ink.

That morning, after watching Sariah unravel in her own house, he came back here and stared at the calendar like it owed him answers.

April 7th.

Last year.

He circled it again. Red this time.

That was the last time they sat together — him, Kris, and Sariah — in the same room.

No weapons. No threats. No fear.

Just bad wine, loud music, and a conversation that ended in laughter.

Before the split.

Before the war.

Before Ade's shadow stopped feeling warm.

Maya showed up at the backdoor twenty minutes later.

No knock. Just presence.

"You marking birthdays now?" she asked.

Spence didn't turn.

"That's not what this is."

"Then what?"

He finally turned to face her. Held her gaze with something that wasn't sadness.

Wasn't regret either.

Just closure.

"It's the last time they were in the same room without wanting to kill each other."

Maya frowned.

"You think they'll come back from this?"

Spence shook his head slowly.

"There won't be another one of those days."

A pause.

Then:

"She's too paranoid. He's too free. And I'm the only one still pretending this family's got anything left but a funeral to plan."

Maya stepped forward, voice quieter now.

"You know what happens next, don't you?"

"Yeah."

He tapped the red circle with one finger.

"Whatever happens, it won't feel like history."

"It'll feel like revenge."

The burner was in a shoebox under Spence's cot.

He didn't notice her take it.

Didn't see her wrap it in a tea towel and slip into the storeroom.

Maya didn't like looking for things she didn't want to find.

But the problem with being smart was you always knew where to look.

She powered it on. No SIM. Just one saved draft in the Notes app.

No label. No date.

Just:

— E. MURDOCH

— D. CLAY

— MAYA TURNER

— J. WARD

— ???

Five names.

All connected. All cracked off different branches of the family tree.

But there was no order to them.

Jon Ward was already gone.

Clay was last seen driving south.

Murdoch was too scared to speak Sariah's name aloud.

And then there was her.

Number three.

The middle.

Maya read it once. Then again.

Didn't blink either time.

She didn't ask who the fifth name was meant to be.

Didn't need to.

Because Kris never wrote lists for efficiency.

He wrote them like scripture.

Not a hit list.

A cleansing.

And she understood the message loud and clear:

If you were ever in the room,

you were never innocent.

She folded the burner into a towel. Slipped it into her coat.

Back at her flat, she pulled out the travel bag she hadn't touched in years.

Started with socks. Then cash. Then a blade she hadn't used since Barcelona.

No fear. No panic.

Just movement.

Deliberate. Quiet. Ready.

Because Maya didn't plan to die.

But she understood now:

Death wasn't the message.

She was.

Chapter 25 - The Funeral We Didnt Schedule

The sky was low that morning. Grey without shape.

One of those East London silences that felt heavier than sirens.

By the time the body was found, the traffic had already been rerouted.

Civilians kept at a distance.

But the whispers were already spreading.

He hung clean.

No rope burn. No bruising on the face.

Just… placed. Lifted.

Like someone had painted the body into the sky.

Vell.

Or what used to be.

He wore the same jacket Sariah had last seen him in — cheap leather, frayed at the cuffs.

Hands folded, not bound.

Pinned to his chest:

A laminated sheet.

One word, thick black ink:

UNTRUSTED

It wasn't scrawled.

It wasn't rushed.

It was printed like a statement. Like a verdict.

Maya arrived before Spence.

She stood back, hood up, sunglasses low.

"This isn't punishment," she said to no one in particular.

A street cop glanced her way.

"You knew him?"

She didn't answer.

She was staring at the handwriting on the note.

The thickness of the lines.

The black ink.

Same as the burner list.

Same as the gun girl incident.

"It's him," she muttered.

The cop looked confused.

Didn't press.

Spence showed up fifteen minutes later, silent as always.

Didn't go near the body.

Just stood beside Maya.

"How'd they get him up there?" he asked.

Maya tilted her head slightly.

"That lamppost was never that tall."

Spence frowned.

"So what, he—?"

"No," Maya said. "This wasn't a hanging."

He stared at her.

"Then what the hell was it?"

"A message."

She pointed to the note. To the perfect edges.

"This was art. Not murder."

Spence swallowed.

"He's not just killing them."

"No," Maya said quietly. "He's curating them."

The burner rang once.

Then silence.

Not even voicemail.

Just the dead, empty "don't try again" tone.

Spence clicked it shut. Tucked it into his jacket.

The street outside was loud, but the inside of The Orchard — the pub Kris once ran before the schism — was empty like it had been drained by time.

Peeling wallpaper. Broken jukebox.

A single bulb still swinging like someone had just left in a hurry.

Spence walked through it slow.

The pub didn't smell like beer anymore.

It smelled like metal. Like powder. Like memory.

The back room hadn't changed.

Round table. Three chairs.

One glass, half-full.

A single bullet casing placed in the centre of the table like an ornament.

Brass. Fired.

.45 — Kris's signature.

Spence didn't sit.

Didn't touch anything.

He just looked around once and said softly:

"Still talking in symbols, I see."

He leaned on the doorframe.

"You want me to know you're still in play. You want me to think you're ahead. But that casing's not fresh."

He pulled out his phone again.

No new messages.

"You're getting theatrical, kid. And theatrical gets sloppy."

A pause.

"Unless you're not sending messages."

He looked at the glass of whiskey.

Condensation gone. The ice melted.

"Unless you're saying goodbye."

Spence stood there a long time, watching the drink like it might move.

But it didn't.

So he turned.

Left the pub.

Didn't lock the door behind him.

The lobby was expensive in that clean, dead-silent way.

Glass walls.

Smooth jazz leaking from nowhere.

Receptionist with perfect posture and no eyes for anything beyond the desk.

Maya spotted Reya instantly.

Corner seat.

Cream coat. Coffee untouched.

Phone face-down beside a keycard.

She didn't stand when Maya approached.

Just nodded once.

Maya sat.

"You picked a nice place to defect."

Reya smiled — thin, not friendly.

"I'm not defecting. I'm evacuating."

Maya crossed her legs.

"There's a difference?"

"There is when you're still alive."

A long pause.

Then:

"I saw your name on the list," Reya said, tapping her nail on the table. "You going to wait for him to call it out loud?"

Maya didn't answer.

Reya pulled a burner from her coat.

Set it gently on the table.

"Here's the deal. You leave with me. Tonight. No calls. No bags. You delete your contacts. You erase your trail. You walk like none of this ever happened."

Maya looked at the phone.

Then up at her.

"And if I say no?"

"Then he gets to you before I do."

Another pause.

Maya leaned back.

"And where exactly are you going?"

"South. Quiet."

"Start a new crew. Different rules. No family. No history."

"No future either."

Reya laughed softly.

"Future's a gamble. I'm after days."

She finished the line like she'd practised it.

Maya tapped her fingers once on the table. Looked toward the lobby window.

Outside, the sky was bruising.

Reya leaned in.

"Pick a direction, Maya. Loyalty's not a virtue anymore. It's a forecast."

Maya stood.

"Forecasts lie."

She walked toward the doors without saying goodbye.

Didn't notice the figure across the street.

Not yet.

The café sat between two shuttered shops on Roman Road.

Didn't serve much. Toasties. Tea. Fried things that all tasted vaguely of oil and yesterday's decisions.

Spence always took the same table. Back left. Facing the door.

Old habit.

The waitress — small, nose piercing, voice like an ex-smoker — brought him tea without asking.

Just placed it down, smiled softly, then lingered.

"You always look like you're waiting for something," she said.

Spence blinked at her.

"Maybe I am."

"Haven't seen you smile in weeks."

"Nothing worth smiling at."

She paused, then asked:

"You believe people can die before they're dead?"

Spence looked at her, surprised by the question.

Didn't answer right away.

Then:

"Yeah. All the time."

"I don't," she said, tapping her pen on the order pad. "Not unless they forget to say sorry."

That made him smile.

Small.

Sad.

But real.

She walked off, apron swinging.

Spence stirred his tea with the same slow rhythm he used when chambering a round.

His thoughts circled like drainwater.

The family wasn't dying.

It had died.

And no one had gone to the funeral.

Only now—

They were finding the gravestones one by one, still warm.

He finished his toast. Left a twenty under the plate.

Didn't wait for change.

As he stepped out, the sky had turned copper-grey.

And somewhere in that colour, he saw the past — still alive, but fading.

Like smoke that never fully cleared.

Maya didn't rush out of the hotel.

She walked like someone who meant to look relaxed, which is always how people look when they know they're being followed.

Her boots echoed against the lobby tiles, her coat too light for the cold — but she didn't button it.

Didn't want her hands hidden.

Outside, the traffic hummed with late-evening fatigue.

Tower Bridge glinted in the distance, all dressed up for tourists who hadn't seen the city rot properly.

She lit a cigarette.

Not for the taste.

Just to have something burning.

Then she saw him.

Across the street.

Lean build.

Black hood.

Leaning against a lamppost like it owed him something.

No movement.

No phone.

No posture shift.

He was facing her.

Just watching.

Maya turned slightly, angling her body behind a parked car, half-shadowed.

She didn't break stride.

But her eyes stayed locked.

And that's when her phone buzzed.

No ringtone. Just the vibration.

One new message. Unknown number.

She stopped walking, thumb hovered over the screen.

Message:

"You're still number three."

That was it.

No name.

No threat.

No punctuation.

She didn't respond.

Didn't look up.

She didn't have to.

Because when she finally glanced back toward the street—

he was gone.

No footsteps.

No sound.

Just an empty patch of pavement…

and a lamppost that somehow looked taller in the dark.

Chapter 26 - Cut From The Inside

The cellar beneath the Queen's Arms hadn't stored liquor in years.

It smelled like dust, gun oil, and moulded concrete.

One naked bulb hung over a steel table.

Cobwebs filled the corners like curtains no one had the guts to pull back.

Kris sat on an upturned crate, one boot propped against the wall, cigarette smouldering between two fingers.

He didn't look up when Kevan "Two-Hour" Shaw came down the steps.

Kevan didn't talk.

Didn't shake hands.

He just stopped three steps from the bottom and waited.

Kris held up the cigarette, tapped ash into an old beer glass, then pulled a folded bit of paper from his inside pocket.

Held it out.

Kevan took it. Opened it.

Three names. One already circled.

Clay Bristow

Maya Turner

Ludo Shaw

Kevan glanced once at the circle.

Then back at Kris.

"Sure?"

Kris didn't blink.

"He's been feeding Sariah. Not just words. Logistics. He got men into my side safehouses."

Kevan gave a small grunt — part curiosity, part disappointment.

"And the other two?"

"Not yet," Kris said. "But they will. Guilt makes people generous. I've seen it."

Kevan folded the paper neatly. Slid it into his coat.

"What's the message?"

Kris blew out smoke.

Didn't smile.

"There isn't one."

Another drag.

Then:

"This isn't about power anymore. It's about rot. I'm cutting it out."

The cellar stayed quiet.

Nothing moved.

Even the shadows held their breath.

Kevan nodded once, slow.

Turned. Climbed the steps.

Didn't say goodbye.

Didn't need to.

Kris stayed seated, finished his cigarette.

When it was gone, he lit another.

One by one.

Like candles for the dead.

The warehouse near Bow was meant for shipping car parts.

Now it held what was left of a dynasty.

Five of them stood in a crooked semi-circle, all different shapes of fear.

Tarn. Elisha. Tonk. Zara. Reg.

All had served under Ade.

All had shed blood for the family.

Now they watched Sariah pace the floor like a surgeon choosing her tools.

No one interrupted.

No one dared.

She stopped at the center.

Chalk in hand.

Bent down.

Drew a slow white line across the cracked concrete between her and them.

Thick. Unbroken. Final.

Then she stood.

"Drin's gone," she said, tone flat. "Not missing. Not in hiding. Gone."

A silence dropped like a sheet of glass.

"He crossed the family. Gambled with lives. With mine. With yours. I asked him to stop. He wouldn't. So I made the choice."

No reactions. Just a shift in Tonk's stance. A tremor in Zara's hand.

Sariah pointed to the chalk line.

"This is it. The cut. You step over it, you're mine. Fully. No doubts. No backdoors. No maybes."

"You stay there—" she gestured to the shadows behind them, "—you walk. Clean. No beef. But you don't get to come back."

No one moved.

Not yet.

Then:

Zara stepped forward.

Then Tonk.

Then Reg.

Then Tarn.

Elisha stayed behind.

Older than the rest.

Wore grief like armour.

Eyes red, hands steady.

"You loved Ade," he said softly. "But you're not him."

"No," Sariah replied. "I'm still breathing."

He didn't argue.

Didn't scold.

He just turned and walked out.

Didn't look back.

Sariah didn't stop him.

Didn't call out.

She waited until his footsteps disappeared, then turned to the others.

"From this point forward," she said, "you speak his name, you follow him, or you even look like regret…"

She dragged the chalk once more — straight through a puddle of leaked oil.

"…you'll join him."

The graveyard behind St. Dominic's was barely a patch of green.

More gravel than grass.

No church bells.

Just pigeons and neglect.

Spence liked it here.

No one followed him to a place where nothing lived.

He didn't come to mourn.

Didn't light candles.

Didn't even visit a specific grave.

He sat on a cold bench under a crooked tree, opened a small black notebook, and began flipping pages.

Not names of the dead.

Names of the living.

A new list.

Zara — still inside

Reya — walking away

Kevan — operational

Maya — volatile, probable exit soon

Kris — moving without orders, pattern broken

Sariah — unpredictable, no blind spots left

A page for each.

Bullet points. Movement logs.

Even estimated mental state — scribbled in shorthand.

Spence had always told himself he wasn't part of the game anymore.

But he was keeping score.

And today, he underlined something he hadn't written before, just beneath Kris's name:

Escalation inevitable. Outcome: fatal.

He stared at the words a long time.

Then he took his pen, clicked it once, and underlined it again. Harder.

The wind moved through the stones like a whisper that no one would claim.

He said it aloud, just once:

"I'm not neutral anymore."

And when he shut the notebook and tucked it into his coat, the air around him didn't feel lighter.

It felt honest.

The road hadn't changed.

It was the houses that looked smaller.

Maya stood across from her childhood home, hands in her coat, a hood pulled low.

It still had the same cracked brick wall out front.

Same rusted gate that used to scream when you touched it.

The door was a new colour — blue instead of red — but the rot was still there, tucked under the paint.

She didn't walk up.

Didn't need to.

This wasn't a visit. It was a pulse-check.

The curtains were shut.

One window had been boarded over.

She counted the seconds between her breaths like someone waiting for a signal.

And then—

Buzz.

Her phone.

No name.

No ringtone.

Just one line:

"He's not your brother anymore."

Maya didn't flinch.

She looked at the screen for five full seconds.

Pressed delete.

Slipped the phone back into her pocket like it had never rung.

But she didn't walk away.

Not yet.

Instead, she sat on the edge of the low brick wall, the one she used to balance on when she was five, arms out like wings.

She looked at the windows.

At the way the rain had stained the house in long black streaks.

Inside that house were memories.

But out here — out here was the truth.

Kris had changed.

No, not changed — evolved.

And Maya wasn't sure anymore whether she wanted to save him…

or stop him.

Either way—

There was no room left for ghosts.

Only the living.

And the ones who needed to die to make the living possible.

It was always going to be Clay Bristow first.

He still moved like he was useful, still picked up his calls on the first ring, still showed up early to everything.

But Kris had already decided.

Loyalty that eager?

It always turned to fear too fast.

Clay left the hospice at 9:13 p.m.

Had just finished dropping a burner package to one of Reya's runners.

The hospital car park was nearly empty — just a few flickering lights, an ambulance at the far end, and the kind of silence that makes sounds louder than they are.

Kevan followed at a distance.

Didn't rush.

He'd done this before — not because he liked it, but because he was built for it.

Clay paused to light a cigarette.

Kevan closed the distance.

Three quick steps.

Silenced Glock.

One shot to the side of the neck — severed instantly.

No blood spray, just collapse.

Clay never even turned.

The cigarette fell from his hand and burned out near the curb.

Kevan didn't linger.

Wiped the grip.

Dropped the casing in a drain.

Walked back the way he came.

⋅

Kris was already outside the hospital morgue, leaning against a brick wall with a newspaper folded under one arm.

He didn't read it.

Just waited.

Kevan approached, slow and dry as ever.

No handshake.

No raised brow.

Kris nodded toward him.

"Did he look surprised?"

Kevan shook his head once.

"No. Looked like he'd been waiting."

Kris pulled a cigarette from his pack.

Lit it.

Exhaled.

"Good."

He didn't thank him.

Didn't smile.

Just took another drag and muttered:

"Let's move to the next."

Chapter 27 - The Woman Who Didnt Flinch

The phone rang once.

That was new.

The first call had come silent, sliding into her inbox like a threat scrawled on a mirror.

This time, it rang.

Proper ringtone. No warning. No lead-up.

Just a single, clear note that snapped through the flat like a starter pistol.

Maya didn't check the number.

Didn't need to.

She answered.

Said nothing.

On the other end—

Silence first.

Three seconds.

Then the voice.

The same low hum. Controlled. Not cockney. Not northern.

Something in-between. Like someone who belonged nowhere but still knew every postcode.

"You're still number three."

Maya didn't blink. Didn't breathe.

"But you don't have to be."

The voice paused like it might add more.

Like it was offering her a shape, not just a warning.

But then—

Click.

Dead line.

No follow-up.

No static.

Just silence.

Maya lowered the phone.

Stared at the screen.

It didn't feel like a threat.

It felt like a door opening.

Or a test.

She didn't call back. Didn't throw the phone.

She just walked to the window and looked out.

The city was soaked and silver.

And somewhere out there, the list was still moving — names rising, falling.

She didn't feel hunted anymore.

She felt…

selected.

The door to the karaoke bar was already unlocked.

Kris didn't knock.

Didn't draw.

Just pushed it open with his shoulder and stepped into a room frozen in some weird, sick version of celebration.

Plastic streamers still hanging.

A glittering disco ball cracked dead in the ceiling.

Mic cables curled on the floor like veins cut loose.

No music.

No speakers humming.

Just one man in the booth —

Ludo Shaw.

He sat on the edge of a leather bench with a can of Fosters sweating beside him.

Didn't look up right away.

Then, without blinking—

"You come to kill me or ask a question?"

Kris stepped forward.

"Depends how fast you answer."

"Fair."

Kris stopped three metres from him.

Didn't sit. Didn't flinch.

Didn't say his name.

"You passed names to Sariah."

Ludo gave a half-shrug.

"I passed warnings. Didn't give up routes or codes. Just told her who'd started looking at her sideways."

"That's enough."

"I didn't lie," Ludo said calmly. "Just wasn't loyal to someone who stopped showing up."

Kris's jaw tightened.

"You think I stopped showing up?"

Ludo leaned forward.

"You vanished, mate. Not disappeared. Not undercover. You just… slid off. No words. No orders. No presence. We were holding together a cracked boat, and you—what? Lit a match and walked away?"

Kris didn't speak.

Didn't blink.

Ludo stood.

Not defensive. Not armed.

Just tired.

"If you came here for a confession, I'll give you three."

Kris said nothing.

Ludo held up a finger.

"One — I tipped off Reya before Clay was dead."

Another finger.

"Two — I thought about selling your address to the Manchester lot. Didn't do it. But I thought about it."

A third.

"Three — I still think Sariah's the better bet."

Kris didn't move.

Ludo took a breath.

"So do it, if you're gonna."

Silence.

Then Kris said:

"Do you know what Clay said before he died?"

Ludo frowned.

"No."

Kris took a step forward.

"Nothing. Didn't even turn."

Another pause.

Then Kris slowly reached into his coat—

Pulled out the burner list. Folded in thirds.

Tossed it onto the booth table.

"Your name's not circled anymore."

Ludo stared at it.

"What's that mean?"

"Means I want to hear number four."

He turned. Walked out.

Didn't look back.

Didn't tell Ludo to follow.

But the door didn't click shut.

It stayed open.

Zara brought the news in without knocking.

Her face was pale.

Phone still in hand.

No mascara this time. No lip.

"Clay's dead."

The words dropped in the room like a small, clean knife.

Sariah didn't flinch.

Didn't ask how.

Didn't pretend to be surprised.

She just looked down at the chalk map still sketched across the floor of the back room.

Marked routes. Drop sites. Weaknesses.

She took a breath and erased two routes with her heel.

Then she stood.

"Get the rest," she said.

⋅

The lieutenants — four now — gathered around the folding table.

Plastic cups. No alcohol. Just tension and too much eye contact.

Sariah leaned her palms on the tabletop and let the silence hang.

"Clay's gone," she said. "And I could stand here and pretend I don't know why, but I'd rather not insult the room."

No one replied.

"He was talking both ways. Everyone knows that. He thought being in the middle made him smart."

She let that sit.

"But middle men die the most quietly."

Still no response. Just Zara shifting in her seat.

Sariah straightened up.

"But that's not the problem."

She stepped back from the table. Began pacing slow.

"The problem is, there's someone else drifting. She's not talking yet. But she's thinking. Watching."

She stopped. Looked around the room.

"Maya."

Tonk looked down at his shoes.

"She's still in?" Reg asked.

"She's still close," Sariah said. "That's worse."

Zara frowned.

"You think she gave up Clay?"

Sariah shook her head.

"I think she doesn't know who she is anymore. And that's what gets families murdered."

She opened the file beside her — Maya's profile. Thin. Precise.

Closed it again.

"I'm not calling a hit. Yet. But I want every pair of eyes watching her. Full report by Thursday."

"What if she runs?" Reg asked.

Sariah smiled. Cold. Shallow.

"Then I know I was right."

The southbound train was quiet.

Rain tapping at the windows. Seats damp with old upholstery and indifference.

Spence sat two rows from the back, coat collar turned up, a worn leather notebook balanced on his knee.

He wasn't headed to a deal.

Not an ambush.

Not surveillance.

Just an apology.

⸱

Jon Ward's daughter lived in a flat above a shuttered print shop in Camberwell.

Twelve years old.

Didn't know how her father had died.

Didn't know why he'd died.

Spence knocked once.

When the door opened, a tired-looking woman with streaks of grey in her roots peered out.

"Yes?"

"Parcel for Isla Ward," he said.

She squinted. "There's no—"

He handed her the envelope. Thick.

Unmarked.

"From a friend of her dad's."

Before she could ask, he turned.

Already walking down the stairs.

She didn't follow.

He didn't expect her to.

•

Back on the train, Spence opened his notebook and flipped to a fresh page.

Drew a line down the middle.

LEFT | GONE

He started filling it in. Slowly.

Not with names — with traits.

Motives. Moments. Things they did or didn't do.

Then he whispered it aloud, not for the first time:

"The wrong people die."

Another line below that, in darker ink:

"That's the only pattern that never breaks."

He closed the book.

Rested his head against the rattling window.

And thought about the day everything had felt simple.

The stairwell smelled like takeaway grease and wet concrete.

Maya's boots echoed up to the third floor.

She didn't rush.

Didn't carry a weapon tonight.

Didn't check the shadows.

She already knew they'd been here.

The envelope was thin.

Wedged neatly under her door.

No stamp. No name. Just precision.

She picked it up, tore it open, pulled out a single photograph.

It was her.

Taken earlier that day.

Crossing the road by the market — same coat, same hair tied back.

Whoever took it had been close.

Too close.

Behind the photo: a number. Burner digits. Handwritten.

Same black ink.

Maya unlocked the door, stepped inside, didn't turn the light on.

She sat on the edge of the bed, the phone resting in her palm like a dare.

Then she dialed.

Three rings.

Then nothing.

Just that same, dry breath on the other end.

She didn't wait for him to speak.

She didn't plead.

Didn't threaten.

Didn't ask why.

She simply said:

"Take me off the list. Or meet me face to face."

Silence.

She held the line five seconds longer.

Then hung up.

No shaking hand.

No deep breath.

She placed the phone beside her.

Laid the photo on the windowsill.

Watched the streetlight blink outside.

And for the first time in days—

She didn't feel like a target.

She felt like the one walking into the crosshairs… on purpose.

Chapter 28 - A Mouthful Of Teeth

The garage smelled of oil and cold metal.

Not the working kind — the rotting kind.

Leftovers from a world that had already crashed once and was ready to go again.

Tonk stood near the shutter, hood down, gloves on.

He wasn't twitchy.

He wasn't wired.

He was careful.

That's what made him dangerous.

Reya came in under the impression this was about a drop.

She was wrong.

The punch came quick — not enough to knock her out, just enough to rattle.

When she woke, she was tied to a folding chair with duct tape looped tight around her ribs and forearms.

Mouth free.

Because Tonk liked conversations.

He stepped into the circle of flickering overhead light, holding two burner phones.

"Guess what I've got," he said, voice mild, almost cheery.

She didn't answer.

He held up the phones.

"One of these is Sariah's. The other's Kris's. They both think I'm loyal."

Reya spat blood.

"You're not that clever."

Tonk crouched.

"You're right. I'm not. But they're that arrogant."

He stood again. Walked a slow lap around her.

"They're gonna kill each other. Eventually. It's baked in. I'm just helping it happen a bit faster. And when they do? There's gonna be land. Broken pieces. Empty corners. Gaps no one bothers to claim."

He crouched again.

Leaning in close.

"I don't want the throne, Reya. Just the land around it."

She glared at him. Face bruised. Eyes sharp.

"Then you're already dead. You just haven't noticed."

Tonk smiled. Stood.

"Nah. I'm just underrated. And that's a beautiful place to live."

He turned.

Left the light behind.

Left her taped up.

Door slammed.

Lock turned.

Reya didn't scream.

She just stared at the floor.

Then slowly…

started working her wrists against the tape.

Maya's flat was quiet, warm, and armed.

Curtains drawn.

Kettle steaming on the hob.

A pistol sat beside her elbow like cutlery.

On the table in front of her—

Three pieces of paper.

Each one a partial list.

Names. Codes. Tags.

Some handwritten. Others typed. One in red ink that smelled faintly like the boot of a stolen Vauxhall.

She'd spent hours comparing them.

Some overlap.

Some oddities.

But only one name showed up exactly once:

Spence.

Not circled.

Not underlined.

Not even marked as urgent.

Just placed—

like a forgotten bullet in the chamber of an old gun.

She stared at it for a long time.

Then folded all three sheets in half.

Twice.

Slid them into the ceramic bowl she'd nicked from a safehouse in Poplar six months ago.

Lit a match.

Dropped it in.

The fire was clean.

Quiet.

No scent except ash and clarity.

Maya watched the flames climb and shrink until all that remained was the warped shape of her own reflection in the bowl's base.

Then she whispered to the empty room:

"No more lists."

And she meant it.

From here forward—

She wasn't cataloguing death.

She was curating it.

The knock came soft.

Not a fist — knuckles.

Spence didn't rush to answer.

Didn't even reach for the blade under the sink.

He waited.

Thirty seconds later, he opened the door.

No one.

Just a folded scrap of paper tucked halfway under the doormat.

He picked it up, unfolded it.

Two lines. Handwritten.

A familiar slope to the letters. A pause between the two digits in the postcode — a habit only Elisha had ever had.

"Peabody Block 9, Unit 6C. Tonight. 10:30."

No signature.

No threat.

No explanation.

Spence stared at it a full minute before moving.

He knew what it was.

A coffin without nails.

⬚

By 10:15, he was walking under the broken streetlights of Lambeth, hood pulled up, breath fogging against the cold.

He didn't carry a weapon.

Didn't tell anyone.

Because some endings didn't need interference.

Just attendance.

At 10:28, he knocked twice on Unit 6C.

The door opened immediately.

Elisha was inside.

Alone.

Hair buzzed short. No drink. No smoke. No gun in sight.

He didn't smile.

Didn't scowl.

Just nodded toward the kitchen table.

"Sit. Got something I want to say before this city buries me."

Spence stepped inside.

He didn't ask what.

He didn't stop him.

He just sat down.

Because that's what you do when the ghosts finally want to speak.

Camden looked grey in the kind of way that had nothing to do with weather.

It was the grey of waiting rooms.

Of apologies never made.

Kris stood outside the assisted living complex, hands in his coat pockets, boots wet from the alley he'd parked in.

He hadn't been here in four years.

Didn't knock.

Just buzzed.

They let him in without a word.

She was sitting at the little table by the window, cardigan folded over her shoulders, her thin white hair caught in the glow of the hallway light.

She looked up.

Didn't smile.

Didn't reach for him.

Just said:

"Did you eat?"

Kris shook his head.

She stood, slowly.

Moved with the careful stiffness of someone who'd stopped rushing decades ago.

Opened the fridge. Pulled out a foil-covered plate. Microwaved it.

They didn't speak while it hummed.

When she set the plate in front of him — sausages, beans, two slices of toast — he nodded once.

"Thanks."

She poured herself tea. Sat across from him.

Watched him eat.

He didn't use a knife.

Just the fork.

Three bites in, she asked:

"Have you found peace?"

He didn't look up.

"No."

She nodded like she'd expected that.

"What then?"

He set the fork down. Wiped his mouth with a napkin he hadn't touched till now.

"Focus."

Her eyes narrowed. Not cruelly. Not surprised.

Just sad.

"And what does that bring?"

Kris took a breath.

"An ending."

She didn't ask whose.

She didn't need to.

When he left, he paused by the hallway.

Looked at the wall where the old photos still hung.

Birthdays.

School uniforms.

Cakes with names on them in cheap icing.

Only one photo had both brothers smiling.

Genuine.

Fourteen and thirteen.

He took it off the wall.

Didn't ask permission.

Tucked it into his coat.

Walked out into the cold.

The tape didn't tear.

It screamed.

Reya had dislocated her thumb five minutes ago, pressing it hard against the edge of the chair until the joint popped like wet knuckle.

Blood ran now.

Not fast — persistent.

She was halfway out of the wrap binding her to the chair, her jaw clenched tight enough to crack.

Another twist.

Another snap.

One finger — middle — bent backward on purpose.

Disfigured, but free.

She didn't scream.

Didn't curse.

Just kept working.

And when her wrist finally came loose—

She stood.

Shaky, leaking, furious.

But upright.

She kicked the chair over.

Walked to the tool rack Tonk hadn't bothered to lock.

Picked the crowbar.

Heavy. Blunt. Honest.

He didn't hear her coming.

Tonk had left the side door cracked.

He was on his phone, back turned, laughing softly.

She didn't say a word.

She swung once.

Crack.

Teeth. Blood.

He hit the ground with a sound that wasn't human.

Then again — across the ribs.

He groaned. Spat. Gurgled something like her name.

She dropped the crowbar beside him.

Leant down.

Close enough to whisper into the mess of him.

"If I wanted the crown, I'd already have it."

She stood.

Wiped her bloody palm on the front of his hoodie.

Walked out.

Didn't run.

Didn't hide.

The night was wide and sharp and waiting.

And Reya?

She wasn't afraid anymore.

She was thinking.

Chapter 29 - No One To Inherit It

The knock on Maya's door didn't sound like desperation.

It sounded like someone who'd made a decision.

She checked the peephole.

Saw the smear of blood down one side of Reya's face.

Opened the door.

Reya stepped inside without waiting to be invited.

Dropped her coat on the floor.

Sat at the table.

She didn't ask for help.

Didn't reach for a drink.

She pulled a folded map from her back pocket.

Laid it flat.

Smoothed it out with one bruised hand.

Maya stood by the sink, arms crossed.

"You look like shit."

Reya didn't smile.

"Yeah. Tonk's not funny anymore."

She jabbed the map with her thumb.

Old borough lines.

Sections marked in faded pen — purple and black ink bleeding into creases.

"They're fighting over these lines," Reya said. "Fighting over bricks and names and who owned what in '09."

Maya didn't move.

"And?"

Reya looked up at her — not pleading, not angry.

Steady.

"And they're stuck. That's why they're dying. They're fighting over what they built."

She leaned back in the chair, blood still wet on her temple.

"We build something else."

The sentence hung in the air like it had weight.

Like it wanted a place to land.

Maya walked over, sat across from her.

Looked at the map.

"What kind of 'something else'?"

"Smaller. Smarter. No names. No symbols. Just moves."

Reya tore the lower left corner of the map off.

Tossed it in the bin.

"No inheritance. Just creation."

Maya didn't nod.

Didn't speak.

She just dragged the map toward her and stared at the blank spot where a territory used to be.

Reya stood. Picked her coat back up. Winced a little.

Before she left, she said—

"You don't have to say yes."

A pause.

"But if you don't say no… I'll come back."

Door shut.

Silence returned.

Maya stared at the map.

She didn't say no.

Kevan didn't like the route.

He'd said so three times.

"Too exposed. Too quiet. Looks like a setup."

Reg shrugged it off like he always did.

Laughed and said—

"Then we're due a surprise party, aren't we?"

They were in the van by 11.

Unmarked.

Silent tyres.

The kind of vehicle no one looked at twice unless it crashed or caught fire.

They were three blocks from the drop when it happened.

A muffled pop —

First tyre gone.

Van slumped sideways.

Kevan hit the brakes.

Second pop — front windshield spidered with a crack.

Then a voice:

"Stay in the van."

Reg didn't listen.

Always moved too fast.

He threw the door open, gun halfway up.

Didn't get a full step out.

A single shot cracked the air.

Clean. Professional.

Reg jerked.

Spun halfway.

Blood sprayed the inside of the windscreen in a tight arc.

His knees hit the curb before his head did.

Kevan dragged him back in.

Hand clamped on the wound.

"Don't move. Don't move. Don't fucking—"

But Reg was already gargling, eyes wide, mouth working at a word he couldn't form.

Then stillness.

Kevan sat there, jaw locked, one hand soaked red.

Gun untouched in his waistband.

The shooter didn't come closer.

Didn't finish the job.

This wasn't about bodies.

It was about messages.

⸱

That night, Kris sat in the back room above Charlie's old boxing gym.

Blank wall.

No distractions.

He took a piece of chalk from his pocket.

Wrote in block letters:

NO MORE SECOND CHANCES

Then underlined it.

Once.

Then again.

Harder.

Until the chalk snapped in half.

The kitchen was too clean.

Not the kind of clean that meant pride —

the kind that meant preparation.

Elisha sat at the table, hands folded.

In front of him, a blister pack of pills.

Next to it, a note Spence didn't read.

He'd seen enough of those.

The kettle boiled behind them but neither moved.

Spence leaned back. Coat still on.

"You brought me here to watch?"

Elisha shook his head.

"Brought you here to tell you something. The rest's just a convenience."

Spence didn't reply.

Elisha opened a drawer. Pulled out an envelope.

Tossed it onto the table.

"In there's a name. You know it. You just don't know who they really are."

Spence didn't reach for it.

Not yet.

"Why now?"

Elisha stared at him for a long time.

"Because a decade ago I sold the wrong soul to save my own."

"Sariah?"

A nod.

"She gave me a way out. I gave her a list. She said she'd burn half of it. She didn't. She used it. Grew from it."

"And the name in the envelope?"

"Someone she never let go of. Someone buried in plain sight."

Spence finally picked it up.

Didn't open it yet.

Elisha reached for the blister pack.

Broke it with methodical fingers.

One pill. Then two. Then three.

Spence watched.

Didn't flinch.

Didn't speak.

Because sometimes the damage isn't in what's done—

It's in what you let happen.

By the time Elisha had swallowed the last one, his eyes were glassing over.

He smiled faintly. Not at Spence.

Just away.

"Didn't want to rot. Just wanted to leave without screaming."

Spence stayed until his breathing slowed.

Until the room was still again.

Then he opened the envelope.

Read the name once.

Twice.

Didn't speak it aloud.

But his fingers curled like a trigger had just been pulled.

The phone call was short.

Zara stepped into the room, phone still lit in her palm, face tight.

"She's alive."

Sariah didn't look up from the reports spread across the desk.

"You're sure?"

"She took out Tonk. Crowbar to the face. Didn't kill him. Made a point."

Sariah flipped a page.

"Good."

Zara blinked.

"Sorry?"

Sariah finally looked up.

"Means she's not just retaliating. She's making a move."

Zara stepped forward.

"So we hit her back?"

Sariah stood slowly, walked to the far wall, opened the small cabinet no one else was allowed to touch.

Inside: a leather ledger.

She pulled it out. Set it down.

Zara hovered, unsure.

"You want to send a team?" she asked.

Sariah didn't answer.

She turned to the last page of the book — blank except for one freshly drawn line.

Then, with a fountain pen, she wrote a single name.

No explanation.

No code.

Just ink.

Zara leaned forward, but Sariah closed the book before she could see.

"We're not chasing Reya."

"But—"

"She wants to build something," Sariah said, walking back around the desk. "Let her."

A pause.

"We'll just make sure the foundation's ash."

Zara stared, waiting for more.

None came.

Just the sharp click of the ledger being locked back into place.

And the quiet certainty of a war being written in pen, not bullets.

The flat was almost bare.

Spence had cleared most of it out — not for escape, just for breathing.

Maya didn't knock.

He didn't ask how she knew where to come.

She walked in.

Sat beside him at the small table near the window.

Between them:

A single sheet of paper.

One pen.

And nothing else.

Spence looked older. Not by years — by weight.

He nodded once, handed her the list.

"You don't have to."

"I do."

He began to read.

One name at a time.

Each name a history. A body. A chain link in the mess they'd both survived.

And for each one, Maya gave the same answer:

"Not worth saving."

He read slower.

She didn't blink.

"Not worth saving."

Another.

"Not worth saving."

She never hesitated.

Never asked for justification.

Just judgement.

Until the last page.

He turned it.

Blank.

The pen hovered.

Maya placed her hand on his.

"This time," she said softly, "we don't write anything down."

He looked at her.

No argument.

No resistance.

Just the long, heavy quiet of two people who finally understood:

Inheritance wasn't coming.

And maybe that was a gift.

Chapter 30 - Nothing But Broken Glass

The desk sergeant at Bethnal Green was halfway through a cold sandwich when the man walked in.

Mid-forties. Leather jacket, bruised lip. Walked like his knees didn't trust the ground anymore.

Didn't ask for a lawyer.

Didn't ask for protection.

Just leaned over the counter and said—

"I'm ready to talk about the Brutalists."

The sandwich dropped.

Ten minutes later, he was in Interview Room 3.

No cuffs. No script.

The detective, a sharp-faced woman named Linton, sat across from him with a pad she didn't plan to write much on.

Not at first.

"Name?"

"Derek Park. Most called me Dee."

"You've got history with the Lambeth crews."

"History's polite. I've got scars."

She flipped through a file. Then looked back up.

"You know how this works. If you're here for a deal—"

"Not here for a deal."

She paused.

"So why are you here?"

He leaned forward.

"You got a pen?"

She handed it over.

He took the notepad.

Started writing.

Name after name.

Crews. Drops. Dates.

Not guesses. Not hearsay.

Details.

By the time he passed it back, her fingers shook.

She stared at the last name:

KRIS.

Underlined three times.

"This is personal," she said.

He nodded.

"My brother. Devon Park. Shot in the back in '13."

"That was written off as crossfire."

"It wasn't. Kris ordered it. Said my brother was late with payment. He was fourteen."

She didn't reply.

He leaned back.

"You don't have to promise me protection. Just bury him. Bury him proper."

Linton looked at the list again.

She didn't smile.

She just stood.

"Stay here."

"Where else would I go?"

The next morning, the information hit Sariah's desk.

She read it once.

Didn't swear.

Didn't react.

She just whispered, almost impressed—

"He did it for free."

And that changed everything.

The Dog & Fiddle wasn't the kind of place you walked into unless you belonged.

Kris did.

Or used to.

Now, he walked in and the room tilted.

Not from the drink — from the silence that followed him.

He sat in the corner.

Back to the wall.

Pint untouched.

Eyes scanning.

Three sips in, he saw the man.

Younger. Hoodie up. Didn't drink.

Kept glancing over the rim of his phone.

Kris clocked the tattoo just under his right ear — barely visible above the collar.

The feather.

Reya's crew.

He didn't ask questions.

Didn't finish his pint.

He stood.

Walked straight over.

Grabbed the kid by the hoodie, dragged him back through the bar.

The few people who might've said something didn't.

Not to Kris.

He shoved open the back door and pushed him into the alley.

The kid stumbled, hands up.

"Wait— I'm just—"

Kris didn't wait.

The first punch broke the kid's nose.

Second shattered a tooth.

By the time the boy tried to run, Kris had already grabbed the broken brick near the drainpipe.

"You shouldn't've been watching," he hissed.

"I wasn't— I was just—"

Crack.

The brick hit skull.

The sound wasn't sharp. It was wet.

Another hit.

Then another.

Until the body stopped twitching.

Kris dropped the brick.

Stared at his bloodied hands.

Then spat on the ground.

Lit a cigarette with trembling fingers.

Didn't call anyone.

Didn't cover the body.

He just walked back inside, ordered another pint, and said nothing.

The next morning, the crew that found the body wasn't Reya's.

It was police.

And the war had officially changed hands.

The warehouse Reya was squatting in used to be part of the old cable yard — a ghost-shell of brick and rust where sound died fast.

Maya arrived through the back entrance.

No headlights. No warning.

Reya was already inside, crouched over a crate with bolt cutters in hand.

When she saw Maya, she didn't smile.

Just nodded toward the bench.

Maya didn't sit.

"I heard about Kris."

Reya shrugged.

"He's a fuse with a gun. Sooner or later, something had to catch."

"He killed a kid," Maya said. "One of yours."

Reya stood. Brushed dust off her jeans.

Didn't look sorry.

"He wasn't mine."

Maya took a step closer.

"You want me in on this? I need to know something."

Reya raised an eyebrow.

"You building for survival… or are you building to burn everything down?"

Silence.

Outside, a lorry rolled up — slow and deliberate.

Reya didn't answer.

She walked past Maya, waved her hand once.

Two of her crew pulled the shutters. The lorry reversed into position.

Tailgate opened.

Inside: crates. Marked with red tape.

Maya's eyes narrowed.

"Is that—"

"From Sariah's own dock," Reya said. "Last night."

She pulled one of the crates open. Inside: high-grade arms.

New, clean, catalogued.

"Half of this city's still playing checkers," Reya said. "I'm already rearranging the board."

Maya looked at the weapons.

Then at Reya.

She didn't speak for a long moment.

Then finally:

"Alright."

She pulled up a chair.

"Let's burn it down."

Zara had done jobs before.

Courier drops. Lookouts. A warning shot now and then.

But never this.

Sariah handed her the address in silence.

A folded card. Red ink. One name.

"One hour. Don't speak to him. Don't let him speak. Just end it."

Zara looked up.

"Who is he?"

Sariah didn't blink.

"Unfinished business."

Zara stared at the card. Knew better than to ask more.

She left without another word.

⸱

The flat was on the twelfth floor.

Empty stairwell. One working lift that screamed like metal dying.

Zara knocked twice.

He opened the door wearing a dressing gown, phone pressed to his ear.

His face fell when he saw her.

Recognition, then confusion.

"Zara? What—"

She raised the gun.

Hesitated.

He stepped back. Hands up.

"Look, whatever she told you—"

She fired.

Once in the chest.

Once in the head.

He hit the laminate floor face-first.

The phone clattered beside him, still connected.

Someone on the other end shouting something distant and meaningless.

Zara didn't look at the body again.

She walked out.

⸱

Back at the house, Sariah was in the garden.

Trimming nothing. Just moving the shears.

Zara stepped into the yard, blood on her boots.

Sariah didn't turn.

"It's done?"

Zara nodded once.

Sariah set the shears down.

Picked up a small black burner from the table. Handed it over.

"Now you're real."

No 'well done.'

No 'thank you.'

No validation.

Just a transaction.

Zara looked at the phone in her palm.

Then back at her.

And nodded.

The knock wasn't loud.

More of a tap — deliberate, soft, knowing.

Spence opened the door without checking.

The corridor was empty.

Just a package resting against the frame.

Brown paper. No tape.

Folded like a present from someone who still believed in rituals.

He bent down.

Picked it up.

Back inside, he set it on the table.

Didn't unwrap it right away.

He stared at it for a long moment —

as if it might make a sound.

Then he opened it.

Inside:

A single shard of glass. Rough at the edges.

Sharp enough to bleed.

He held it up to the light.

The back was scratched — not deep, but deliberate.

One word.

Etched with something brutal:

SPENCE.

No threat. No warning.

Just the reminder of a name.

He turned it over.

Saw his own reflection in the curved fragment.

Only half his face fit.

The rest was just light and distortion.

He pocketed the shard.

Didn't bandage the cut it left on his thumb.

Didn't throw it away.

Because he knew—

This wasn't a threat.

It was a trigger.

And the next move wouldn't come from a rival.

It would come from the part of himself he'd been pretending didn't exist.

Chapter 31 - There Is No Clean Up Crew

Rain tapped lightly on the windscreen.

Just enough to blur the edges of everything.

Kris sat in the driver's seat of a borrowed Golf.

Engine off.

One hand on the wheel, the other curled in his lap like it didn't belong there anymore.

The car smelled of blood.

Old blood.

His sleeves were still damp with it — from the pub, from the alley, from the brick.

He hadn't changed.

Couldn't.

The hospital loomed just across the street.

White lights. Blue glass. A revolving door that spun too fast, like time didn't care.

Inside, she was pushing.

He knew that.

He'd dropped her at A&E himself.

Watched her vanish behind a nurse with gloves already snapped on.

She'd turned to look at him once.

Not to say anything.

Just to check if he'd follow.

He hadn't.

Now he sat.

Silent.

Shaking, just a little.

Not from fear. Not from weather.

Just from the way his hands wouldn't clean.

He checked his phone.

One message:

"7lbs 3oz. Boy. Doing great. Wants his dad. – Nurse Amari"

Kris stared at it.

Typed:

"I'll be better later."

Then paused.

Backspaced the last word.

Typed it again.

"Maybe."

He didn't press send.

He just locked the screen and dropped the phone into the footwell.

Outside, a couple laughed as they walked past the car, umbrella spinning.

Kris lit a cigarette with fingers still cracked at the knuckles.

Blew the smoke toward the windshield, not the window.

And said, softly, to no one:

"I'll see him when I'm clean."

But he didn't know what that meant anymore.

And even if he did—

He knew he wouldn't be.

The meeting was held in a laundrette.

Still open.

Still running.

Washing machines thudding a quiet war-drum while a pensioner folded towels in the corner.

Maya sat in the back booth, counting coins she had no intention of using.

Reya stood by the window, hands in her coat, one eye on the door.

Then he walked in.

Briggs.

Once muscle for the Manchester crew.

Tall, broad, face like busted clay — one of the old hitters who'd survived too many shootouts and kept all the wrong lessons.

He saw Maya.

Didn't flinch.

Saw Reya.

He paused.

She'd put a bullet through his shoulder two years ago.

He sat anyway.

Maya offered no handshake.

Just words:

"We're not here to say sorry."

Briggs smirked.

"Didn't expect you to."

Reya spoke next.

"We're not offering a truce. We're offering land."

Briggs frowned.

"Why?"

Reya slid a folded street map across the table.

South of Vauxhall. Two blocks. Clean and unclaimed.

"Because the ones in charge are still drawing lines in blood. We're offering ones in ink."

Briggs didn't move the map.

Maya said:

"You want a piece of something long-term? This is it. You run it clean. No crosses. No chaos. You're not answering to us, you're partnering."

He scratched at his beard.

"This is coming from you two?"

Reya nodded once.

"We build different."

A long pause.

One washing machine beeped.

The pensioner looked up. Then back down.

Briggs looked at the map again.

"And if I say yes?"

"Then you get out of the way when the walls start falling. We're not saving anyone still inside."

He stared at them for a long moment.

Then picked up the map.

"I don't say no to second chances."

He left without looking back.

Reya exhaled.

Maya watched the door swing shut.

"That's the problem with promises," she said.

"They take longer to load than guns."

Reya didn't reply.

But she knew Maya was right.

And somewhere behind that knowledge was the sound of Sariah getting ready to reload.

Maya was already waiting when Zara slipped through the back gate of the allotment.

She'd picked the spot herself.

No cameras. No street view.

Just garden beds and a half-dead lemon tree leaning in the wind.

Zara didn't say hello.

Maya didn't stand.

They sat at opposite ends of the bench.

Like strangers killing time.

Like traitors trying not to get caught.

"You weren't followed?" Maya asked.

Zara smirked.

"If I was, you'd already know."

Maya nodded once.

Waited.

Zara pulled out a folded sheet of notepaper from her jacket.

No name on it. No logo.

Just a series of numbered drop points — warehouses, storage units, dead bars — all marked as quiet.

"That's where she's hoarding."

Maya took it without a thank-you.

"This is intel."

"No. This is a warning."

Zara stood.

"You think I'm switching sides?"

Maya looked up at her. Calm.

"Aren't you?"

Zara's voice dropped.

"I'm not switching. I'm preparing."

She stepped away, halfway to the exit before she added—

"I'm not waiting to be inherited."

Maya didn't reply.

She folded the paper once.

Twice.

Then pocketed it.

She didn't know if Zara was an ally, a plant, or a fuse.

But the truth didn't matter yet.

The truth would show itself in the smoke.

Clapham hadn't changed.

Not really.

New paint, sure. New chain cafés.

But the bones were the same —

old skin with cleaner clothes.

Spence stood outside the block for a long minute.

Didn't smoke. Didn't pace.

Just stared up at the fourth floor, where a light flickered in the leftmost window.

The shard in his coat pocket felt heavier than it should've.

He took the stairs.

The smell hit first.

Dust, bleach, and burnt toast — the scent of a place that hadn't been abandoned, just forgotten.

Flat 4C.

The door was open.

Not wide.

Just cracked — the kind of invitation that didn't ask.

He stepped inside.

The layout hadn't changed.

Living room to the right. Kitchen straight ahead.

And there, above the broken dresser — the mirror.

Or what was left of it.

A jagged hole where the shard had once been.

Edges raw, brown with time.

Then the voice:

"Didn't think you'd come back."

He turned.

Jess stood in the doorway to the kitchen.

Older now, tighter around the eyes.

But the same girl who used to sit on the arm of Devon Park's chair, calling bullshit on half the room.

She didn't smile.

Didn't move.

Spence swallowed.

"You sent it?"

She nodded once.

"Thought maybe you needed reminding."

"Of what?"

She walked in, sat on the edge of the couch.

"What you left behind when you chose silence over truth."

Spence didn't sit.

"Devon got caught in—"

"Devon was left to die in a stairwell while you ran messages for Kris and his little empire."

"I didn't know he was—"

"You didn't ask."

Silence.

She pointed at the mirror.

"That used to show people who they were."

"Now?"

"Now it shows what's missing."

Spence reached into his coat.

Pulled the shard.

Fitted it into the gap.

It didn't sit right — not anymore.

Neither did he.

Jess stood.

"I'm not asking you to make it right."

"Why send the glass then?"

"Because someone's about to lie about the past again," she said. "And I thought maybe, just maybe, you'd finally do something else."

He didn't speak.

She walked out.

And he stayed there, staring at the warped reflection of a man shaped by what he refused to see.

The fire had gutted the building three days ago.

Not arson.

Not retribution.

Neglect.

Sariah stepped over the threshold of what used to be a safe house.

Now it was ash and steel, curled from the heat, the smell of burnt plastic clinging like sweat to the air.

She didn't bring security.

Didn't call anyone ahead.

This place used to house seven people — maybe more.

Now it echoed with nothing.

No tags.

No blood.

No messages.

Not even a claim.

She walked slow.

Boots crunching across blackened floorboards.

Bent down.

Picked up a piece of melted phone casing. Still warm from the sun.

This place had meant something once.

A checkpoint. A fallback.

Now it was a footnote.

She lit a cigarette.

Hands steady.

No shaking now.

No flinching.

She stared at the far wall where names used to be spray-painted.

Crew roll calls. Birth years. Slashes through the dead.

Now it was soot.

A puff of wind stirred the air. Carried the ash toward her.

She stood still.

Let it hit her.

Didn't brush it off.

Just said softly, almost without sound—

"It's just us now."

Not a cry.

Not a threat.

A diagnosis.

There was no one coming to clean this up.

No one to avenge it.

No heirs.

Just the ones still breathing, still walking.

Still fighting each other.

She left without another glance.

And the ash fell behind her like snow that didn't melt.

Chapter 32 - The Last Problem

The message came folded in half, no envelope.

Spence found it on the hood of his car, held down with a cigarette butt still warm.

He read it twice.

Didn't need to read it a third time.

He found Kris half-drunk in a flat that used to be someone else's — now just a mattress on a floor and curtains made of bin liners.

"It's from her," Spence said, holding it out.

Kris didn't take it.

"What's it say?"

"She wants to meet. No crew. No guns."

Kris lit a match off the carpet and dragged it across the rim of a cigarette already frayed from his teeth.

"So she's finally grown the spine to do it herself."

Spence didn't smile.

"The place she picked… it's the old butcher's off Railway Street."

Kris exhaled smoke.

That place — the one with freezer doors rusted shut and a trapdoor in the back room.

The one they used to run out of when this life still felt like family.

"You goin'?" Spence asked.

"She's not gonna talk me down."

"She's not gonna talk at all, Kris."

Kris stood, slow.

His side still bruised from a job gone bad three nights ago.

He picked up his pistol from the milk crate and checked the mag.

Spence frowned.

"Thought it was no weapons."

Kris holstered it.

"It is."

"Then why bring one?"

"Because I know her."

He walked past Spence, grabbed his coat, stepped into the street.

Didn't look back.

The butcher's was just as they'd left it:

padlock sawn through, air stale with ammonia and rot, the paint peeling off the tiles like old scabs.

Kris stepped inside, boots echoing.

No lights.

Just moonlight slicing through slats in the boarded windows.

She was already there.

Back to the far wall.

Hands in her coat.

No words.

He didn't reach for his gun.

Not yet.

She didn't move either.

They just watched each other — the silence between them not awkward, just heavy. Like a rope pulled tight.

Finally:

"You look like shit," she said.

Kris shrugged.

"Been seeing my family lately."

She tilted her head.

Eyes cold, unreadable.

"You think this is how it was supposed to go?"

"I think you wanted this before Ade was cold."

"I kept it together."

"You ripped it apart and called it structure."

"I built something."

"You buried everyone to do it."

Her lip curled.

Not a smile.

An old wound opening.

"You were always soft, Kris. Always leaning into someone. Ade. Me. That woman who left you."

He stepped closer.

"You stabbed us all in the front and still called it loyalty."

She didn't flinch.

"You think you're better?"

"No. Just finished."

She reached into her coat.

Kris froze — half a second from drawing.

But it wasn't a gun.

It was something smaller.

Shinier.

He caught the glint just as she twisted her shoulder—

The blade wasn't big.

Three inches, curved, handle wrapped in tape.

But it was enough.

Sariah moved fast —

No hesitation, no warning.

She lunged like someone trying to end a decade in one motion.

Kris staggered back, too late.

The knife went in.

Low. Left side.

Not deep enough to drop him — but close.

A fire lit behind his ribs.

His knees buckled.

She came again —

Striking fast, aiming high.

He caught her wrist mid-air, slammed her into the freezer door with a crack of shoulder bone on steel.

She grunted, brought her knee up into his thigh.

He folded forward—

She grabbed his head, tried to slam it against the tile,

but he twisted at the last second and sent her into the floor.

They both fell.

Rolling.

He reached for her wrist again — the one with the blade.

Blood smeared her forearm.

Couldn't tell if it was hers or his.

She gritted her teeth, snarled:

"You should've stayed gone."

He hissed through blood in his mouth:

"You should've brought a second knife."

She almost laughed.

Then punched him in the wound.

He gasped — vision flickering.

But his hand found something—

The inside pocket.

Cold metal.

The pistol.

He got the barrel up under her chin—

She knocked it sideways.

The shot fired wild — shattered tile.

She straddled him, raised the knife again.

His left hand came up — blocked the swing.

His right found the gun again.

And this time—

He didn't miss.

Sariah froze.

The pistol pressed hard against her forehead, just above the brow.

Her breath hitched.

Not from fear —

From realisation.

Kris's face was pale, slick with sweat, jaw locked.

He was bleeding badly now.

Still holding her down with one hand, the other tight on the trigger.

"Go on then," she whispered.

"Finish what you started."

Kris didn't answer.

His eyes never left hers.

Her lip twitched —

Not regret. Not even hate.

Just pride. Twisted and burning.

"Told you. You were always soft."

Kris leaned in, blood dripping from his chin.

"Not anymore."

And then—

BANG.

One clean shot.

The sound snapped through the butcher's like a slammed vault door.

Sariah's head jerked back.

Her body went limp immediately —

No twitch, no sound.

Just a final breath forced from her lungs as if it had been waiting all this time.

Her eyes stayed open.

Kris didn't move for a moment.

Just stared.

Then he shoved her body off, slowly.

Rolled to one side.

Groaned as the knife wound screamed.

Blood seeped down his side like ink into paper.

He looked at her again.

Still.

Red pooling under her skull.

Nothing left to say.

The butcher's door swung open with a long metallic groan.

Kris stepped into the cold air, one hand pressed to his gut.

Blood soaked his shirt, dripping into his waistband, trailing behind him.

No lights.

No sirens.

Just the buzz of a faulty streetlamp and the soft rumble of distant traffic.

He didn't look back.

Not at the butcher's.

Not at her.

Just forward.

Every step was pain.

A slow, dragging rhythm — like a man trying to outrun his own name.

No one followed.

No one waited.

The estate ahead looked hollow.

Windows like dead eyes.

Shutters closed.

Streets emptied out, as if the city itself had stepped back to let him pass.

He moved through it like a ghost that hadn't decided if it wanted to stay.

His hand slipped from the wound once.

He caught it.

Grimaced.

Kept going.

Past the place where Ade used to stand with a burner phone.

Past the alley where Drin once bled out under neon.

Past it all.

Until finally—

He stopped.

Halfway down the block.

Breathing ragged.

One hand resting on the old brick wall like it might remember him.

The wind picked up.

Kris turned his face to it.

Eyes closed.

Then opened them.

And whispered, not to anyone alive:

"There's nothing left to inherit."

Then he walked on.

Into the dark.

Alone.

Bleeding.

Free?

Unclear.

Printed in Dunstable, United Kingdom